LOVE SELDOM.
TRUST NEVER.

TY MARSHALL

For information contact : info@tymarshallbooks.com

TYMARSHALLBOOKS.COM
Book and Cover design by Pixill Designs
ISBN: 9780998441979

First Edition: Month 2013

10 9 8 7 6 5 4 3 2 1

LOVE SELDOM.
TRUST NEVER.

EMMETT,
THANK YOU FOR
SUPPORTING. STAY BLESSED
HOPE YOU ENJOY!

PROLOGUE

East was a man of little patience as he looked down at his watch, he had to control his frustration. It was almost midnight and he was tired of waiting. In his eyes, tardiness showed a lack of discipline. It also was a sign of disrespect. "What the fuck is taking this nigga so long?" he sighed while lowering the music. East clenched his jaw and scanned the block. He was alone in his car, across the street from Liberty Square, or as it was called by everyone, Pork & Beans projects, with a Glock .40 resting on his lap. In front of the apartments sat a cluster of wilted stuffed animals, their once vibrant colors now faded. Candles, empty liquor bottles and crosses anchoring a makeshift memorial. A constant reminder of the violence that plagued the neighborhood. Shit was real in Liberty City and East wasn't trying to get caught slipping.

Before he could begin his next thought, East spotted the person he had been waiting on. They were strolling towards him like they didn't have a care in the world, carrying a black bag full of money. What had once been a fresh, white wife beater covered the young man's slender, tattooed body. His long, thick dreads bounced with every leisure step he took. It was like he was moving in slow motion.

East lowered the window of his old school Chevy, letting the pungent smell of weed escape into the night air. He stared the man squarely in the eyes, visibly irritated by his lack of urgency. "Damn my nigga, you're acting like I got all night," he said as they slapped five. "You know I hate that shit," he explained, taking the bag from the man's outstretched hand.

"My bad homie," the man answered.

"I gotta count this shit or is it all there?" East asked.

"It's all there?"

East noticed the man wouldn't make direct eye contact with him. His lethargic speech and body language made it clear that he was high on more than just weed. "You gotta lay off the lean. That shit got you off point. You can't be moving like a snail out here. Especially when you carry my money," East advised.

So many thoughts were racing though the man's mind that he couldn't form the words to reply. Years of trust and loyalty between the two of them mere seconds away from being broken. The coldness of his gun had grown warmer against the small of his back while he'd nervously paced back and forth inside the apartment. That's what had took him so long. Even now, he was biding his time, waiting for the perfect chance to put his murder game down. For a killer, timing was everything. He no longer saw a friend when he looked at East. He saw opportunity. The chance to move up a few rungs on the street ladder and take better care of his daughter. At least that's what had been promised to him. East was in the way of all that.

When East turned away to sit the bag on the passenger seat, the timing was perfect. The man stepped closer to the car and in one motion pulled out his gun, pressing it to the back of East's skull. There was one last message to deliver before he sent a bullet through his brain.

"Dos said, it ain't nothing personal. You just in his way," then he squeezed the trigger.

LOVE SELDOM. TRUST NEVER.

PART I: WINS & LOSSES

ONE: TEN YEARS EARLIER

The black s600 Mercedes-Benz maneuvered through Liberty City as the smooth sounds of John Coltrane's Naima filled the interior. Ricardo sat silent in the backseat, serious and in deep thought as he stared out of the window. His business was finally on the verge of expanding but something didn't feel right. Something was lacking. Respect, he thought to himself. So, he decided to call a meeting to iron out a few issues within the city. His operation had recently suffered a big loss. A shipment had gone missing, leaving him without product to move and in debt to his connect. His gangster was being tested. His reputation was on the line and he needed some answers not only for himself but for the connect as well.

His vehicle pulled up to an abandoned meatpacking plant in the industrial part of the city. It had once been a thriving business until the recession hit and the economic decline forced its doors to close permanently. Now the plant was abandoned and overrun by rodents. However, there was business still being conducted within its walls, street business. The bloodstained floors told stories of the meatpacking plant once housed there but also of the meetings that had gone terribly wrong there. Ricardo had recently purchased the property with plans to bring jobs back to the community. As he passed through the gates, he began moving his fingers as if it were him playing the saxophone on his favorite part of the song. He preferred to handle business smoothly like the jazz he enjoyed listening to often. He wasn't interested in warring over turf. That would only leave a trail of bodies in the streets and bloodstained sidewalks in the city. He didn't need that type of heat. That wasn't his style. He was a technician not a brawler, same way he had been as a former boxer. But a line had been crossed and boundaries needed to be established, so things could continue to run smooth amongst the hustlers in the city. When the car came to a stop, his henchman got out and walked around to open his door, allowing him to step out. When Ricardo entered the building, all eyes landed on him, but no one said a word. His posture was strong, upright with squared shoulders. He was dressed in a black Brioni suit. His whole aura embodied power and the entire room felt it. He was a boss in the making. A man on the come up. He took his time before speaking, pacing back and forth, looking into the eyes of each man in attendance. Finally, he looked over to his right-hand man Tez, who was standing near the guests of honor. Six men. Each a top hustler from the city, were on their knees, hands and feet bound with duct tape, burlap bags covering their heads. Ricardo gave Tez a nod and he started pulling the bags off the men's heads one by one, revealing their mouths were also duct taped. Their moans filled the air. Their pleading eyes landing on Ricardo as he stared down at them with no mercy. Somebody had violated him. His thirst for revenge so strong that simply killing whomever was responsible just wasn't good enough. It was about respect and their lack of it had earned them all a place there. Ricardo wanted to set an example for the whole city of hustlers who wasn't taking him seriously. *Former professional boxer turned drug dealer*, they laughed behind his back. He heard the whispers but after today there would be none. He hated that it had to come to this, but it was a necessary evil of the drug business. The streets owed him a debt. They were about to pay up, in blood.

"Gentlemen, y'all are here today because you all have a piece of something I want," he said staring into each one of their eyes. "Since Old Man Al passed, the crown in this city has been broken up in too many pieces. It's time to put an end to that. I've been patient. At first, I tried to be peaceful. I approached each of you with an opportunity. The chance for us all to work together in harmony. But one by one you all turned me down," he explained, his hands behind his back as he walked around them. "Then somebody got the bright idea to take something that belonged to me," he exhaled and shook his head. "But it's ok," he said rubbing his hands together. "This is what we're gonna do."

On cue, Tez stepped around, pressed his gun to the forehead of one of the men on their knees and pulled the trigger.

BOOM!

The gunshot echoed through the empty building. The groans and muffled pleas of the other men grew louder. But their sobs and begging to be spared fell on deaf ears. They were at the point of no return.

"Gentlemen, don't beg," Ricardo instructed. "Have some pride," he said as Tez moved down the line putting bullets in all their heads.

BOOM! BOOM! BOOM!

When the last man was dead, Ricardo walked out the building, Tez at his side, leaving his henchmen behind to grind up the dead bodies.

"We still got one loose end to tie up," Tez reminded him.

"Don't worry, I didn't forget," Ricardo declared, giving himself the once over, making sure there was no blood splatter anywhere on his suit. Checking his watch, he realized, *they were running late.* There was more unfinished business to attend to. He quickly slid into the back seat of the Benz and shut the door. "Hey, be quick but don't hurry," he instructed his driver as the luxury car pulled away. He was on his way to another funeral.

CHAPTER TWO

East stared at the open casket as he sat on the edge of the wooden church pew, his hands resting on his legs. He wore a white dress shirt that was buttoned uncomfortably tight around his neck, a black tie and an oversized blazer that had been hand me downed from one of his older relatives. His slacks were high water, barely long enough to cover the thick pair of white sweat socks and cheap dress shoes he wore. Still, his eyes never strayed from the face of the man lying in the casket. At 14, he had already been to too many funerals to keep count. Still, he'd never seen a dead body up close before today. He had always managed to keep his distance from the front of the church during funerals. Instead allowing others to grieve over the dead bodies of their loved ones. But this was a body he couldn't avoid. This time he was required to sit on the front row, right beside his mother, Ebony, who offered him comfort by continually rubbing the middle of his back. This time the body wasn't a family friend or some upstanding member of the community who required that respect be paid to them. The body in the casket belonged to his father.

The church was crowded. Crying faces filling every row, most of them belonging to beautiful women his father had been in some form of a relationship with. One woman sat in an adjacent pew, dressed in all black, holding a screaming toddler. East was certain the baby belonged to his father. The woman's eyes were hidden behind dark shades to conceal her pain, but her tears still made a trail down her face bringing her mascara with it. The deceased man taking with him a piece of her heart.

The walls of the church were lined with neighborhood dope boys dressed in dark clothes, their heads bowed, their talking restricted to muffled hisses. Their eyes glued to the floor, unable to look up at the man many had known since childhood.

East paid little attention to those around him. Instead, his eyes remained on the waxy glaze of his father's face. The caked-on makeup gave him an artificial gleam. Strangers would constantly stop East in the streets and tell him how much they looked alike. He could never see what they saw. Maybe his hatred wouldn't allow him to. But as the pastor began to read from the scripture, East allowed his thoughts to drift. He was no longer in the stale smelling church with tidal waves of sadness all around him. His mind was in another place, which allowed his expression to be free of emotion. That lasted for as long as it took for the pastor to finish his eulogy and it became his turn to speak. His mother nudged him out his trance. East took a deep breath before rising to his feet. Releasing his mother's hand, he walked towards the casket as the church grow quieter. The crying seemed to be replaced with gasps of amazement. Even the woman holding the toddler lowered her shades to get a clearer view of him. His resemblance to the man in the casket was undeniable to all in attendance.

Truthfully, East would have preferred to be alone in that moment. Allowed time with his father in private. Without all the crying and stares of strangers. He wanted to speak words only meant for his father's ears. It was something he'd never gotten the chance to do while he'd been alive. East would've loved the opportunity to do so now. Sadly, he would forever be denied that. The man in front of him had been mostly absent from his life. East knew stories but he had so many questions of his own. Ones only his father could answer. Now he was being asked to speak in front of everybody. To say his final goodbyes to a man he knew very little about. In front of a group of faces, most of which he didn't even know.

The heavy odor of the fluids and powders the undertaker used made East's nostrils burn. He stood over the casket studying his father's face and for the first time, he allowed himself to see their resemblance. The dead man was handsome like himself, just darker. The suit he wore did little to hide his muscular build. However, it did cover the bullet holes that had sapped the life from his body. Shots fired by a person who would never be arrested for the crime. Even at his age, East understood the world he lived in. It was a world a child his age should have feared, yet he was strangely drawn to it. Both consciously and subconsciously, East knew that murder was a natural by-product of the drug game. The *kill or be killed* mind set was as intricate a part of Miami as its beautiful beaches and palm trees. Shootings weren't uncommon in his Liberty City neighborhood, which was one of the poorest. Neither were the people who looked the other way and the secrets that were kept for decades. In ghettos of Miami, those who ran their mouths to the police received a harsh and brutal punishment. East didn't know why his father had been killed but like everyone else, he'd heard some things.

For most of his life, East hated the mere thought of the man. Now, he found himself with a bunch of what ifs. A lump formed in his throat, the kind that was usually followed by tears. Thoughts of the unfulfilled relationship between the two of them was the cause. *What boy didn't want a father?* East was no different, no matter how much he tried to suppress the yearning. He wasn't sure who to feel sadder for, himself or his father. He lowered his head, squeezing his eyelids tight, refusing to let the tears in the wells of his eyes fall. Confusion surged through his body. He'd been so used to controlling those emotions, that it felt weird being on the verge of crying. He'd always had to be tough, not only for himself but for his mother as well. He was her protector as much as she was his. That's what had been taught. That's what she always preached. Toughness.

"You're a young black boy from the ghetto. People will always assume that you're weak and dumb. Let 'em! Use it to your advantage cause nobody in this world is gonna cut you any slack or feel sorry for you. So, tuck them damn tears." Her words replayed in his mind.

His mother, Ebony was all he had and vice versa. Although they didn't have a lot, they had each other and that was enough for them. *So where were these sudden feelings for his father coming from? Why did he feel an ounce of love for a man who'd never showed him any?* It didn't make sense. His young mind had no answer, only more questions and confusion.

East reached in his pocket, removing a folded note and slid it into the inside pocket of his father's suit. It was written the night before, filled with all the things he'd intended to say. Things he wished he could say to him; good and bad. East decided against sharing it with the church. It wasn't their business. It was between him and his father. He made a silent vow to allow all his ill feelings to go in the ground with the dead man. Even though something like that was easier said than done. It was good enough from him. East decided to skip out on a speech all together. He patted the note in place, looked in the casket one last time then turned down the aisle and walked out the church.

"East, are you okay?" a sweet voice called out

from behind as he exited the church. "East, hold up." He paused. When he turned, Samayah was walking quickly towards him with a look of concern on her young pretty face. "Are you okay?" she repeated.

"Mhm," East swiped his nose and nodded his head, but she could tell he wasn't.

"If you need to talk about it, we can. If you want to," she offered.

East took his time replying. He paused because a part of him wanted to talk about what he was feeling. He just wasn't sure what that was. He was still trying to process it for himself. Samayah was just trying to help. She meant good. He knew that but sharing his confusion with her or anybody wasn't something he was interested in doing now. Although young, East knew to protect his thoughts and guard his secrets closely. That was something he would continue to do throughout his life.

"Nah, I'm okay. For real," he replied, letting her down easy.

"Are you sure?" she pressed, disappointment sprouting on her eyes.

Samayah couldn't help it. She tried not to let his refusal affect her, but it did. Recently, everything East said or did affected her in one way or another. Her teenage heart was on a rollercoaster every time they shared the same space. If he smiled, she blushed on the inside and butterflies fluttered in her stomach. But the slightest sign of rejection, like right now, him not wanting to share what he was feeling, would demoralize her. What frustrated her most was that he didn't even notice it. None of it.

"Damn, sis," her twin brother's voice interjected as he emerged from the church behind her. "The nigga just said he's aight. Leave him alone."

"Ain't nobody talkin' to you, Sameer," she snapped, elbowing him in the side.

He grunted from the blow, "Chill out," then laughed. "I was just playing. Real shit though bro, you good?" he asked East.

"Yeah. I'm good," East eyes lowered to the ground. "I just wanna take a walk, that's all."

"You want me to roll wit' you?"

"Nah. It's cool. I'll be back in a few, in case my mom asks," East replied evenly, no emotion present as he walked away from them.

The twins belonged to Ms. Ang, who was East's mother's *fast-talking* best friend. Although they were twins, they were complete opposites in every aspect. Sameer, who everyone called Screw, had the lighter complexion of the two. He was handsome, tall for his age and slim. Although they were mixed, Bahamian and Dominican, his features were more Dominican, rocking his long hair out and curly. Despite the suit he wore, Screw looked like trouble on two feet to everybody that saw him coming. He'd earned the nickname from people around the neighborhood, who said he must've had a screw missing in his head to do some of the crazy shit he did.

Samayah on the other hand had honey brown skin with amber colored eyes. Her round cheeks fit her chubby face perfectly. She was sweet but feisty, while still being shy and a bit of a nerd. Although she was a cute girl, she was going through the awkward stage of becoming a teen whose looks hadn't come together yet. She always kept her head in a book, like the copy of *The Hunger Games* she had tucked in her hand at that moment.

Screw stood in front of the church, watching East disappear up the block. He heaved a sigh. "See you done ran my nigga off," he teased.

Samayah sucked her teeth "Boy bye," she countered before heading back inside the church to find their mother, bumping him as she passed.

CHAPTER THREE

"You okay, baby?" Ebony asked then kissed East, leaving traces of her lipstick on his cheek.

"Why does everybody keep asking me that?" he asked, a hint of annoyance in his voice as they entered the community center in the projects for his father's repast.

Ebony turned to face him. Using her thumb, she rubbed the lipstick off his cheek. "Be nice," she reminded him, like the loving mother she was.

Although money was always in short supply, love never was with her. Ebony made sure to spoil East with affection. Teaching him the value of being a good man, being respectful and honorable. She wouldn't allow their harsh surroundings to influence his moral compass. She was grooming a strong black man and knew those life lessons were important for him to have. She was raising him but in a strange way, they had kind of grown up together.

Ebony James came from a wholesome family. The baby and only girl of three children. Her parents were both good, hard working people who were well liked in the neighborhood. Everybody knew her father Eddie by his stout, muscular frame. Remembering when he was a promising running back at Miami Northwestern High School. Ebony's mother, Gayle was an attractive woman who maintained the athletic figure she'd gotten from playing basketball and volleyball at the same high school. The couples mutual love for sports had brought them together and it became the thread that bounded the James' household together. Ebony wasn't immune. Like her mother, she was very beautiful. Having the kind of alluring features that drew attention to her wherever she went, even as a teenage track star at Miami Northwestern. She was a 5'6" redbone bone with freckles and perfectly proportioned curves and curly black hair that flowed down to her shoulders. Her pretty brown eyes could pierce into the gaze of any man and drive him crazy.

So high school boys didn't stand a chance with her back then. Not only was Ebony blessed with good looks, she had brains to match and a heart of gold. She was on the fast track to college.

However, the summer before her junior year, Ebony's heart was captivated by a handsome, smooth talker named Derek Eastwood. He was tall, handsome and dipped in chocolate with a street edge. It was the sense of forbidden danger that appealed to Ebony's youthful innocence. Three years older and much wiser to the ways of the world, his charm proved to be irresistible. It didn't take long before Derek got in her head, then her heart, and finally in her pants.

After an evening of laughs and sipping Thug Passion together. Derek skillfully made passionate love to her for the first time. Taking his time to educate Ebony about her body. Teaching her the art of sex.

After that first summer night, Ebony was hooked, wanting to spend every wakened moment with him. Indulging in sex session after session. Derek was her drug and she was chasing the first high every time they made love. Every time the sex exceeded the last time. Every orgasm better than the last one. Ebony always needed more. Derek had unleashed a beast.

she thought was in her future. Her taking his last name. Eastwood James was born.

It would be six long years before she seen or heard from Derek again. By then, their son was walking, talking and looking more and more like him. Derek never denied East. Although, he would be in but mostly out of his son's life until the day he died. Leaving Ebony with the sole responsibility of raising their child.

"I love you, baby," Ebony voice cracked as the memory faded, tears coming to her eyes as she stared at her son.

East looked into her eyes and noticed that they were becoming moist. He watched as the tears formed and slowly fell onto her cheeks. He hated to see her cry. Sometimes wondering if he was the reason, she was always so sad and stressed. Maybe it was his fault, that she struggled to make ends meet. Maybe he was the cause of all her pain.

The sad truth was that Ebony was struggling with something much bigger than East could fathom. She didn't even have a full grasp of it. Mental illness, more precisely, depression. She'd suffered in silence for years. Too ashamed to seek help or confide in anyone or fully accept it. Even her co-workers weren't aware of what was going on. That's because she had mastered the art of deception when it came to her mental health. Able to mask what she was dealing with well. Ebony would go from crying spells to angry outbursts and anxiety attacks, then back to a stable emotional state, all in one day. Her erratic emotions then easily explained away to others by blaming PMS or being a black woman with an attitude. She was always prepared with an excuse but lately it had become increasingly harder for her to justify. Her mood swings were occurring more frequently. She lacked an appetite and the weight loss was noticeable to others, especially East. He didn't know what it was, but he knew something was wrong. His normally loving mother would become so irritable for what seemed like no reason. Ebony was a social butterfly but now she would seclude herself in her room, never opening the blinds to allow light in for the whole weekend. East could hear her crying in her bed at night and wondered why. It made no sense to him, but he didn't speak on it. *Stay in a child's place. What happens in this house, stays in this house,* he had always been taught, two common rules in black households.

"Don't cry, ma," he embraced her tightly, her head laying on his chest. He already stood taller than her, something he had inherited from his father too.

"I love you too."

Ebony felt his hand delicately wipe the tears from her cheek. She forged a smile and they stood quietly staring at each for a moment. When she looked in his face, she saw a younger version of the man that lay dead in the casket back at the church. After all these years, Ebony had never loved another man the way she loved Derek. He was her first love and would always be. The good and the bad. No other man had ever compared to him. She attempted to break eye contact by looking away, but East grabbed her hand. His expression becoming curious as he examined her face.

"What's wrong, baby?" she asked him.

East exhaled, "Ma, are you crying because you still loved my father?"

Ebony was caught a little off guard by his question. It was like he had read her mind. East never ceased to amaze her. He was so sharp for his age. She paused before answering, pondering how to explain something so complex as love to a 14-year-old. Ebony decided it was best to be honest. She reached out and grabbed both of his hands. "Real love. Real true love," she emphasized. "The kind I once shared with your father; it never dies. It never completely fades. It's like he gave me a blood transfusion and he'll forever run through my veins and here," she touched her heart. "So, yes, I was and still am," she answered truthfully. She could instantly see East wasn't pleased with her reply.

His brow lowered. "Why? He ain't never did nothing for us, ever. That's not love ma. That's not what a real man does. A real man handles his responsibilities and takes care of his family," he declared. "Ain't that what you always taught me?" His voice wasn't loud, still his anger was evident.

East treasured the ground his mother walked on. It had been a struggle for her raising him alone. A teenage dropout in the projects, on welfare, with nothing but an eleventh-grade education. Ebony had exceeded expectations and was doing the best she could. She had gotten her G.E.D and completed 10 months of courses at Everest Institute to become a medical assistant. She had earned everything she had the hard way. East never saw her flaws when he looked at her, only her triumphs and her strength. He admired her so much, loved her even more. She was godly in his eyes. He vowed to do whatever necessary to protect her and change their living conditions, first chance he got. She deserved it and he felt he owed it to her. His father had gotten off easy. East could and would never respect that.

Ebony smiled. She was amazed at how quickly he was becoming a young man. It made her proud. "Baby, I know it's hard for you to understand right now. But I'll always love that man because he gave me the greatest thing, I have in this world…you," she confessed, caressing the side of his face, looking in his eyes. "I want you to remember what I'm about to tell you. And I want you to hold on to it. You were made out of love. And despite what you may hear in the streets about your daddy, that ain't your cross to bear. That's what he did. That's not who you are. Only you decide that. You hear me?" she said.

East admired her attempt to cast his father's actions in a good light, but he knew better. Still he respected the effort she made enough not to respond. Instead, he placed a gentle kiss on her cheek, offered a half-hearted smile before walking out of the front door of the community center. He was content to avoid the flood of visitors bearing food, sympathy and fake well wishes.

Outside on the steps of the community center, East sat alone, watching a group of teenagers playing basketball in the park. He undid the first few buttons on his shirt as he took in his surroundings. Cars zoomed up and down the block. People were going about their day like everything was normal. Nothing had changed in their world. Death only affected those connected to the dead. Life went on for the living. In that moment, East found clarity in his own thoughts. Nothing had really changed in his life either. He couldn't miss what he never had. He couldn't mourn Derek Eastwood. He had no connection with him. *He doesn't deserve my tears,* East thought as he looked down at his shoes, never noticing the man approaching.

"Hey lil' man," a husky voice called out to him, grabbing his attention.

East looked up, immediately recognized the man standing in front of him, dressed in a customized bespoke Brioni suit, Christian Louboutin suede derby shoes and wearing a Gold Rolex. It was hard not to know who he was; Ricardo Wheeler was a pillar in the Liberty City community. A local legend revered by the entire city. The former middleweight boxer had been an alternate on the '96 Olympic team in Atlanta and was a middle of the road contender as a pro. After his career ended, Ricardo poured back into the community that helped raise him. Opening a boxing gym, where he taught local kids the sweet science. He owned a small grocery store, a clothing store, barbershop and other real estate. He was loved by many and known to rub shoulders with some very important people around the city. There was even a sign that read, "Welcome to Liberty City, the hometown of Olympian Ricardo Wheeler," when you entered city limits. He was a shining example of someone that had risen from the ashes of the crime and poverty that had ravished the city and become successful.

Ricardo removed the dark shades from his face to get a better look at the kid on the steps and couldn't believe his eyes. "What's your name lil' man?" he inquired sizing East up. When the young man hesitated to answer, Ricardo tried to ease his apprehension. "I'm only asking because you look exactly like an old friend of mine. I was wondering if you're related to him?" he explained. The way Ricardo spoke was smoothly southern. His words were deliberate and polished with only a hint of a twang.

"Oh yeah?" East replied, still not willing to fully engage.

"Yeah," Ricardo chuckled at the kid's reserved demeanor. It was a bit standoffish, but it was to be expected. Liberty City bred toughness and made people guarded. "Derek Eastwood. You know him?"

"Knew him, you mean, right?" East corrected.

"Right." Ricardo agreed.

"Nah, I didn't...but he was my father."

Ricardo began to nod in confirmation. *Ain't no denying that shit,* he thought to himself then flashed a disarming grin. "You look just like him," he stared. "Especially back when we were your age. Whatchu about 12, 13?"

"14," East replied, resting both arms across his knees and straightening his back. "So, how well did you know him?" he asked, his curiosity peaked a bit.

"I would say really well. I wouldn't be alive if I didn't," Ricardo recalled. "Me and your daddy went way back. He helped me out of a bad situation, once or twice, back in the day. I had to come pay my respects," he admitted, continuing to eye the young man in front of him. If Ricardo didn't know any better, he would have sworn his old friend had spit the little nigga out.

East hated for someone to say that he resembled his father. Even more so now that there were rumors about Derek working with the feds against some major players. Word on the street was that's why he was killed. East didn't know if the gossip was true or not, but he didn't like the thought of it. Nobody wanted to be the son of a snitch. It was a lifetime scar East surely didn't want to wear. No matter how his mother tried to sugarcoat it. Still, to see Ricardo

Wheeler there to pay his respects was a pleasant surprise. He had no idea the two men had known each other. Then again, he didn't know who his father had known.

"If you don't mind me asking," Ricardo probed, "Who's your mother?"

Before East could answer, a black Mercedes pulled up to the curb and captured his attention, drawing his eyes away from Ricardo. When it came to a stop, a medium built man exited from the passenger side and walked over to Ricardo. He was dressed casual not in a suit and wore no gaudy jewelry, just a gold Rolex as well. He had butterscotch skin, a low cut with faint waves and his facial expression was like stone. Far less welcoming than Ricardo's was. He glanced at East then leaned in, whispering something into Ricardo's ear. East couldn't hear what was being said but noticed the slight change in Ricardo's facial expression as he listened.

When Ricardo turned his attention back to East, the smile returned, "Tez, you'll never guess whose son that is, right there," he stated proudly. Tez examined the young boy's face. A hint of recognition instantly surfaced in his gaze. Ricardo's smile widened, knowing Tez was seeing what he had already saw. "Yeah, crazy right?" he confirmed without Tez having to respond. "Now, who you said your mother was again?" Ricardo asked East.

"Her name is Ebony," he replied.

"Ebony?" Ricardo repeated slowly. His head tilting and eyes looking upward, trying to place the name with the face. He couldn't, he was drawing a blank. "Ebony?" he snapped his fingers.

"He talkin' bout Tweet, for Pork and Beans," Tez reminded him. His voice was raspy, unforgettable after you heard it once. It sounded like it hurt him to speak, like there was sandpaper in his throat.

"That's Tweet's son? Get the hell outta here," Ricardo couldn't believe it. His voice unable to hide his surprise. *No wondered that nigga D used to always be in the projects. That nigga was fuckin' fine ass Tweet back in the day. He had to be the first nigga to crack the seal on that pussy,* Ricardo thought to himself, a slight grin creasing his lips.

"You know my mother?" East asked in an overly protective manner, addressing the smirk on Ricardo's face.

"I know your whole family. They're good people." Ricardo claimed. He hadn't lied.

Tweet had always been a respectable female with a good reputation from a solid family. When she dropped out of high school and popped up pregnant, it was like it came out of nowhere. Nobody even knew she was having sex or with who. For Ricardo, it had stayed that way until that very moment.

"We gotta slide," Tez uttered with a bit of urgency. A reminder to Ricardo of the business that needed to be handled.

"Lil' man," Ricardo called out, rubbing his hands together. "You should ask your mother if you could come by my gym sometime," he offered. "Maybe I can teach you how to throw a punch and tell you some stories about your daddy from back in the day," he laughed reminiscing. "Nothing like what these niggas saying about him now," Ricardo rubbed his hand over his beard.

"I don't care about what nobody got to say," East hid his lie well, pretending the rumors didn't bother him.

"That's good. Stay like that. Never worry about what a nigga gotta say. Especially if it ain't putting no money in your pockets," Ricardo schooled. East caught the jewel and nodded. Ricardo reached into his pocket, pulling out a knot of money. He peeled off a few hundred-dollar bills and walked towards East. "Here, make sure your mother gets this. Tell her, I'm sorry I couldn't stay but I send my condolences." He placed the crisp bills into the young man's hand. "Come see me at the gym, um," he paused, pointing and snapping his finger, realizing he never got the boy's name.

East caught on quick, finally ready to offer his name. He calmly said, "Everybody just calls me East."

Ricardo smiled hearing the name. "I'm gonna keep an eye out for you, East." Then he got into the backseat of the waiting car. Tez hopped back in the passenger side and they pulled off.

CHAPTER FOUR

Ricardo relaxed as his Mercedes-Benz cruised on I-95. His driver didn't need instruction nor directions. He knew where to go. He had made the trip several times before. After exiting the highway on to the streets, they turned onto Collins Avenue and drove a few blocks before parking behind a smoke grey Maybach S62 with the curtains closed.

"Stay here," Ricardo told Tez as he calmly exited the Benz, holding two black leather Cartier bags. When the Maybach's trunk popped open, he placed both bags inside and carefully closed the trunk. Then he walked around and got into the backseat of the car. Two Latino men sat inside. One behind the wheel, and the other, an older man, sat in the backseat.

"Ricardo my friend, it's always a pleasure to see you," the older man said extending his hand.

"You too, Mr. Navarro," Ricardo replied as they shook hands.

Jose Navarro, a Hialeah businessman, was Ricardo's connect. A Cuban refugee, Navarro was the liaison in Miami for a powerful Mexican cartel. But no one would ever know it by the way Navarro carried himself. Short in stature and soft spoken, he hid in the shadows, deep inside corporate America. In fact, he was a well accomplished businessman. He owned a chain of pharmacies that carried his name, coffee shops and restaurants and many other residential properties in and around Miami. But behind all his legal businesses, Navarro was a very powerful man in the underworld.

"How's that beautiful new bride of yours?" he asked holding on to Ricardo's hand firmly, refusing to release it. The car grew tense in an instant. The man behind the wheel locking the doors, all while keeping his eyes focused out the window.

"She's doing fine," Ricardo answered, remaining calm. He didn't crack easily under pressure. He understood the line of questioning from Mr. Navarro. It was a subtle threat. A message from the cartel. An indication of their displeasure about the missing product. It also was a warning that Navarro wouldn't accept any excuses for a lack of payment. There would be a price to pay and it would be with blood. Ricardo's and his family. Despite his accountant like appearance, Mr. Navarro was ruthless. He stared into Ricardo's eyes, searching for weakness but found none. Satisfied, he released his hand.

"I always liked her," Navarro recalled with a smile then got right to business. "The people I work for really appreciate the job you did for them, taking care of that little problem," he said. "But, this thing now, with the shipments," he shook his head. "It can't—"

"And it won't," Ricardo interrupted. "It was a one-time thing, but it's won't be a problem anymore," he assured.

"What assurance do I have of that?"

"My word is more valuable than any assurances I can give you," Ricardo stated confidently.

Navarro smiled for the first time. "So, that's everything?" he asked about the bags in the trunk.

Ricardo shook his head, "To the last penny."

Mr. Navarro nodded respectfully. "I must admit, I'm very impressed. I underestimated you. I expected you to come with excuses."

"You shouldn't have," he said then smirked. "When can I expect the next shipment?"

"Very soon. A day or two."

"Perfect. Thank you," Ricardo replied. After shaking hands again, he opened the door and stepped out. Mr. Navarro watched him walk back to his vehicle and get inside. When Ricardo pulled off, Mr. Navarro signaled his driver to pull off in the opposite direction.

When Ricardo returned home, he shut the door and headed straight to the master bedroom. Inside the room, his beautiful wife, Lauryn, was lying naked across the large king-sized bed. A few lit candles sat on opposite sides of the bed, filling the room with the aromatic fragrance of apple blossoms. Ricardo stared lustfully. From head to toe, Lauryn was the most beautiful woman he had ever laid eyes on. He felt like the luckiest man in the world. She was younger than him, only 22. Although he was 32, she kept him feeling youthful. He had to stay in fighting shape just to keep up with her in the bedroom.

"Are you gonna stand there staring at me? Or are you gonna do something about it?" she teased, rolling on to her back. Lauryn leaned against a pile of pillows and spread her legs open. She waved him to her.

Ricardo's erection grew as he watched her suck on her finger and began rubbing on her clit. He quickly undressed out of his suit and joined her on the bed. He trailed kisses up her leg to her midsection until he reached her pierced navel. Circling his tongue around her navel, dipping it in and out as Lauryn began to moan. As Ricardo licked upward, he found her erect nipples. He began sucking on them, a pleasure point he knew she loved.

"Oh, baby," Lauryn moaned as he nibbled harder on her puckered right nipple.

He flicked his tongue over the sensitive spot and sucked harder and harder. He could hear the faint rhythm of her heartbeat grow louder and stronger. Ricardo moved to the left nipple, roaming her body until his hands were on her firm ass. He glided his tongue down to her wet pussy. He palmed her ass cheeks. Lauryn moaned softly as he thrust his tongue into her wetness then flicked his tongue on her clit. With his forefinger and thumb, he penetrated her a bit and then slurped her clit until it became harder.

"Don't stop! Suck it right there, daddy," Lauryn pleaded, grabbing the back of his head, making certain he didn't move. It was nothing like getting her pussy ate. Chills surged though Lauryn's body as her orgasm built. "Ooh ... oh ... oh," she groaned, pulling

Ricardo's head deeper into her wetness as she exploded. Ricardo emerged from between her thighs with her juices dripping on his lips. Lauryn pulled him up to where his mouth met hers. She slid her tongue into his mouth, circling his lips with the tip of her tongue then made sucking motions that took his breath away.

Ricardo couldn't take it any longer. He wanted to be inside her. With no wasted motion, he penetrated her pussy with his rock-solid dick. Lauryn screamed his name as he entered her. Ricardo was like a beast, pounding her wetness with powerful strokes.

"Fuck me harder daddy," Lauryn begged, spreading her legs into a V and grabbing her ankles. She was taking all his dick deep inside of her pussy. Ricardo was fucking her like he wanted to tear her a brand-new pussy and she loved it. "Oh, I'm cumming," she screamed as she exploded all over his dick. Her sexy screams sent Ricardo's body into overdrive. He felt his climax approaching like an out of control train on the train tracks. He couldn't stop it if he wanted to. He bust his nut inside of her then collapsed into a panting, sweating heap. By the time Lauryn's breathing slowed down and her heart stopped trotting, Ricardo was ready to go again.

* * *

East laid awake in his bed staring up at the ceiling. He couldn't seem to fall asleep. His thoughts were racing. The chance meeting with Ricardo Wheeler heavy on his mind. He couldn't shake the feeling. It was a yearning, a need to know that wouldn't go away. Ricardo had known his father. They shared a friendship. He knew things about him. Information he was willing to share with East. No one had ever offered that. Not even his mother. She could only tell what she knew and that wasn't much. They had only shared a summer together. That wasn't long enough to get to know anybody. East couldn't deny his interest. It had been a long day, but he was looking forward to the chance to talk to Ricardo again. As time passed his thoughts began to calm. He rolled on to his side and noticed his mother at the door, peeking in on him. "Hey ma," he said.

Ebony pushed the door open slowly. "Boy, what are you still doing up at this time of night?" she asked, making her way to the edge of his bed.

East shrugged, "I don't know. I couldn't sleep."

She took a seat next to him, "Why, are still thinking about the funeral," she reached out and ran her fingers through his curly hair.

"No not really, just thinking," His voice was pure. His eyes still held a child's innocence in them.

"About what then?" Ebony questioned her brow wrinkling.

"Nothing in particular. Just regular stuff," he replied hoping to avoid having to tell her actually what was on his mind.

"Ok. What kind of regular stuff?" she pressed knowing her son better than he knew himself.

"Man stuff. You wouldn't understand," he chuckled.

"Oh yeah?" she laughed with him. "Boy, please. You ain't no man yet," she said.

"I am the man of this house," he joked, puffing his chest out.

"Oh yeah?" Ebony said then began tickling him. East began to scream in laughter. "See!" she teased, "You still my little baby," She laughed. "Now take your butt to sleep before I...whip...that...ass," she joked, tickling him with every word.

"Ok. Ok, ma, chill," he begged unable to stop himself from laughing.

Ebony's smile stretched from ear to ear. "Goodnight," she kissed him before getting up. She fixed his covers on top of him before walking towards the door. She paused when he called out to her.

"Ma," East shouted leaping from the bed.

Ebony was startled. "What boy?" she asked nervously.

He walked over to his dresser, opened the top draw and retrieved the money Ricardo had given him. "I almost forgot about this. Here, this is for you."

Ebony looked down at the large bills that he stuffed in her hand then back up at him with raised eyebrows. She turned her head to the side. Her motherly instincts kicked in immediately. "Where'd you get this money from?" she demanded to know.

"Ricardo Wheeler, you know, the boxer dude—"

"Yeah, I know who he is," Ebony said cutting him off. "But why did he give you this money?"

"He gave it to me for you," East explained. "I saw him outside the community center today. After the funeral. He said he knew my dad and told me to tell you, he was sorry that he couldn't stay."

Ebony had a look of confusion on her face. "I didn't know he knew your dad."

"He said, he wouldn't be alive if he didn't. Something about my dad helping him back in the day," East recalled.

"Oh...ok," she said suspiciously. "That was really nice of him." *Lord knows we can use it around here*, she thought the last part of her statement to herself.

"He wants me to come by his boxing gym to talk

to him," East said.

"No, I don't like you fighting as it is. Now you want to be a boxer. No, that's not safe," she quickly dismissed like an overprotective mother would.

"C'mon ma. It'll give me something to do. Instead of being around here, hanging in the projects with Sameer and Que all day," he tried reasoning with her.

"I'll think about it."

"Pleeeease."

"I said, I'll think about it," she repeated but a little less stern.

East grabbed her hands, "Please ma," he laid his natural charm on thick.

Ebony couldn't deny that face. "Ok. Now go to bed," then she walked out the room.

CHAPTER FIVE

Prince guided his BMW through traffic, heading for a strip club on 79th Street called the Foxxy Lady. When he entered, strippers were bouncing and shaking their asses as Rick Ross' *BMF* blared out the speakers of the dimly lit club. He moved through the spot like he owned the place. This was his home away from home. Prince wasn't for the glitz and glamour of some of the other strip clubs in Miami. He didn't like surgically enhanced women. He liked fat asses with stretch marks and big titties with natural sag. Prince was a hood nigga to the core. He was in his element at the hole in the wall spots. If he couldn't get in with his gun, he wasn't coming in. There were no bottles being popped in here, just niggas with bottles of beer and plastic cups filled with Hennessy. Thick clouds of cigarette and weed smoke gave the spot a gloomy look.

Tonight, Prince was looking to blow off some steam. He could have easily called one of the many bitches in his phone. After all, he was a one of the top hustlers in the city. He had coffee brown skin, long curly dreads that lay on his broad shoulders and a muscular frame. He looked like he played for the Dolphins. But he was there because of one stripper in particular.

Prince approached the bar, greeting the bartender. "What up, homie?"

"My nigga Prince, what's good wit' you?" the dude behind the bar asked back.

"Same ol' shit. You see Dream fine ass?" he asked cutting straight to it.

"She around here somewhere," the bartender shrugged his shoulders.

Prince glanced around the club. Five girls were working the floor. One of them, Jade, spotted him at the bar and her heart leaped in her chest. Not from love and not for him, but for the money she'd been offered to make a call, the moment she spotted Prince in the club. He had a price on his head. He was looking like a lottery ticket to her and she was about to cash in. She kept an eye on him. *Niggas out here looking for him. And he just walkin' around by himself like it ain't nothing. This bout to be the easiest two bands I've ever made*, her pussy got moist from the greedy thoughts in her mind. She slipped away from her lap dance and rushed to make that call. It rang a few times.

"Who this?" Tez's raspy voice came through the phone.

"This Jade."

"Jade who?" he asked, wondering how some random female had gotten his number.

"Jade," she repeated, "from the Foxxy Lady," sounding a little disappointed that he didn't recognize her.

"Oh ok. What up?" he asked, uninterested in whatever the reason she was calling for.

"I caught that fish you were looking for," she said.

Tez sat up in his bed. He knew exactly what she meant. "Where at?" he asked with murderous intentions.

"Here, at the club. He just walked in and he's by himself," she explained, ready to cash in her lottery ticket.

"Make sure he don't leave," Tez ordered and hung up.

Jade strutted across the floor to where Prince was standing at the bar. She brushed her naked body against him from behind. He turned around. When he noticed it was Jade and not Dream, he looked annoyed.

"Bitch, if you don't back up off me and get the fuck out my face," he arrogantly spewed, turning away from her.

"Damn boo, it's like that? A bitch just trying to show you some love," she insisted.

He laughed. "Bitch, your little scrawny ass can't do nothing for a nigga like me."

"I can show you better than I can tell you," she purred, sliding her hand over the front of his pants, grabbing his dick through his jeans. "Believe me, I know what to do with all that."

"Nah. I'm good," he knocked her hand away. "Now get the fuck out my face," he dismissed her by waving his hand.

Jade sucked her teeth. "Whatever."

"Exactly," he said turning his back to her.

"I got something for you. Bitch ass nigga," she mumbled under her breath as she walked away.

"Anyway. What were you sayin' my nigga? Prince asked as he picked back up on the conversation with the bartender.

"Oh yeah, I heard niggas hit ol' boy for a six pack," gossiped the bartender.

"Who you talkin' bout?"

"The nigga Ricardo."

"Oh word?" Prince pretending to be surprised by the news of the stolen bricks. "Who was it?" he asked but he already knew the answer. It was him.

"All I heard was niggas caught him slippin' and got him. Took everything," the bartender explained, while cleaning off the bar.

Prince shook his head and shrugged his shoulders. "This game ain't for everybody." They both laughed.

"True," the bartender agreed.

The way Prince figured it; Ricardo didn't deserve his respect. He wasn't a street nigga. He was the city's golden boy. A has been boxer that was trying to infringe on what he had established. Prince planned to punish Ricardo every chance he got, until he ran him completely out the game. He turned and scanned the club again. A smirk spread across his face when he finally spotted Dream emerge from the dressing room. He rubbed his hands together in anticipation, imagining his dick inside her wet mouth.

Dream was the baddest bitch in the club. She

wasn't the prettiest, just the sexiest. She had a cute face and a round ass. But her most attractive feature was her big, pretty, pillow lips. Men's dicks stiffened just from staring at them. Dream was a seductress, licking her lips and flirting to drive them crazy. She put her luscious lips to good use. Her head was lethal. Her rep legendary. She could suck a quarter out of a parking meter. That's what kept Prince coming back. He decided to play the bar for a few more minutes, ordering a second drink. When Dream spotted him from across the club, she smiled with thoughts of milking his big dick. She sashayed over to him.

"Hey daddy, you always looking so good," she said, tracing her hand across his cheek.

"You too ma," Prince said, grabbing her hand and making her twirl for him. He smacked her on the ass. "You know I had to come see you."

"I know. I've been missing you," she flirted.

"Show me then," he said, downing his cup of Henny in one gulp. He got up from his seat and Dream led him to the back of the club just as Tez was pulling up outside.

Prince entered the private room behind Dream and sat down on the leather sofa. He searched his pockets for his lighter. He found it and lit the blunt in his mouth. Dream closed the curtains behind them. The song changed to something with a slower tempo and she began moving her body to the music. Slow and seductively, she started to remove her clothes until she was completely nude. She walked to him like a sexy kitten, switching her ass as she moved towards him. Dream undid his pants and lowered to her knees. She took his gun out, sitting it on the floor next to her. She reached into his boxers and released his erect dick. She looked him in his eyes and licked her lips before taking him deep into her mouth. Prince's head fell back, and his eyes closed from the warmth and wetness.

Jade sat at a secluded table in the smoky club, focusing on the entrance to the private rooms. A bouncer was posted up in front. Suddenly her phone buzzed. She looked down at the text message, it was from Tez. *I'm at the back door*, it read. She slid out her seat and strutted over to the bouncer.

"Hey baby," she flirted with the big, burly man as he eye fucked her. "I left something in one of the rooms back there," she said.

"No problem, ma," He didn't even question it, stepping aside letting her pass.

Jade winked at him. She crept along the wall and hurried to the back door. Nervous energy surging through her body. She unlocked the door and opened it, allowing a mask wearing Tez to step in.

"Where he at?" he asked looking around, making sure no one was around.

"He's in there," Jade pointed to one of the rooms. Tez went to move pass her but she stopped him. "You gonna take care of me, right?" Jade inquired, dollar signs dancing in her greedy eyes.

"I already told you that. Now go back out to the club, we'll talk later," he said seriously, not interested in going back and forth about it. As she went to creep away, he grabbed her arm tightly, "Keep your mouth closed," he warned her. The look in his eyes told Jade that if she didn't, she'd be joining Prince on his permanent vacation. Tez released her arm, then crept towards the room.

Inside Dream was deep throating Prince. He palmed her head as her warm, moist mouth covered his whole dick. Chills began running through his body. He released the weed smoke from his lungs into the air. "That feels good, ma," he choked out his words.

Dream enjoyed hearing him and took her time. It was intense and the more he enjoyed it, the wetter her pussy became. Dream was making passionate love to his dick, using only her mouth and showing off her deep throat skills. She took his dick deeper inside her throat until she started to gag. That only made Prince more excited. He moaned.

Tez heard the moans and smelled the weed. He peeked into the room. Prince's eyes were closed as Dream's head bobbed up and down. Tez spotted Prince's gun on the floor next to her. He smiled and screwed a silencer on his gun as he stepped inside the room. He had truly caught the nigga with his pants down.

Prince was in heaven as Dream sucked his dick. He could feel his body on the verge of an explosion then suddenly, she stopped. Prince opened his eyes to see why and found himself staring down the barrel of a .45 silencer. Two bullets ripped through his head. Two more ripped through his chest. The lit blunt fell from his hand as he slumped in the chair.

Dream cowered against the wall, grimacing at the sight of Prince's dead body. She went to scream but it got caught in her throat when Tez aimed his gun directly at her. He put his finger to his lips and shook his head back and forth. Dream knew exactly what he meant. Before she could acknowledge it, Tez was already gone. Leaving her paralyzed in fear but thankful for her life and Prince another unsolved murder.

CHAPTER SIX

Two days passed before East wandered into Ricardo's boxing gym on 17th Avenue. He would have gone the very next day but didn't want to appear overzealous to a man like Ricardo. Even at his age, East could recognize power when he seen it. The black Mercedes-Benz was on display right in front of the gym. Parked where everyone can see it. Spotting the beautiful vehicle, made East's heart rate speed up a bit. Anxiety surged through his body, making him question if he really should be there. *Did he want to know more about his father? Or more about Ricardo Wheeler?* Truthfully, a little of both had led him there. Ricardo had a magnetic aura. A powerful charm and

East's intrigue had created the perfect storm.

Once inside, East played the cut, fading into a corner to watch everything from afar. He felt nervous and excited at the same time. He leaned against a wall, taking in his surroundings and listening to the unfamiliar sounds of the gym. The grunts of the fighters, the thuds from the gloves hitting punching bags and the hiss of the rope being skipped. It was all new to him. Even the scent of the gym was unlike anything he had smelled before. It was a distinct odor of sweat and leather, spit and blood.

After spending time observing, East began to make his way around the gym. He wanted to get a closer look at everything. He kept looking around, searching the gym with his eyes, hoping to spot Ricardo. He wasn't having any luck laying eyes on him. Finally, he decided to entertain himself. He spotted a vacant heavy bag and walked over to it, throwing a couple light punches. The bag swayed back and forth slightly. East threw a few more, these were a little harder causing the bag to rock more. He grabbed the bag with both hands, stopping it. Looking around, he noticed a group of kids, ranging in all ages, standing near the ring. They were all in awe of the young fighter inside the ring. He looked about a year or two older than East. He moved gracefully, throwing combinations as the trainer called out number combinations. The sound of his punches echoing off the pads when they landed, sounding like tree branches snapping. East recognized the trainer. It was the man that had accompanied Ricardo to his father's funeral. East studied the two in the ring, soon finding himself mirroring their routine. Memorizing it easily, he threw the punches as they were called out. He was captivated by the atmosphere. Unbeknownst to him, Ricardo had eyes on him from the moment he entered the gym. Watching his every move on the cameras from his office. Tez lowered his puncher's mitts and turned towards the group of teens gathered around the ring.

"Hey, any of y'all wanna get some work in?" he asked. His hoarse voice, overpowering every other sound in the gym without having to scream.

The teens went silent. Their apprehension thickening the air as the tension built. *Why ain't nobody raising their hand,* East asked himself, scanning the boys' faces for would be challengers. Now the whole gym grew quiet. You could hear the tick of the clock on the wall damn near. Still, no one accepted the challenge. With no one volunteering to spar, East stepped forward, "I do," he declared, walking towards the ring as every eye in the gym fell on him.

A slight smirk appeared on Tez's face. He was a man of few words and even less emotions, but he admired East's fearlessness. Tez looked towards Ricardo, who was now standing in the doorway of his office with eagerness in his eyes. He nodded, giving his approval. The fighter in the ring was his son, Ricardo Jr., affectionately known as Dos. He was the best young prospect in the gym. There would be no better way to see what East was made of than to throw him right into the hottest of fires.

"Tez, that's my lil' man from the other day," Ricardo yelled across the gym. "Get him some gear. Let's see what he's got." His words caused a complete frenzy. Kids began racing to the ring apron, gathering around, clapping their hands and chanting.

"Dawg fight! Dawg fight!" they cheered.

"Man, that kid is crazy..."

"No one can beat Dos..."

"Yeah, Dos bout to fuck lil' homie up," a chorus of voices said throughout the gym as East made his way through the crowd.

East never wavered. He climbed into the ring and Tez began fitting him with the proper equipment as the chants grew louder. East had never worn headgear, a mouthpiece or gloves before. The equipment felt heavy on him. *How can someone fight with all this on?* he wondered. He had never been inside a ring either, but he had more than his share of fistfights in the neighborhood. He wasn't scared of anyone. There was no bitch in him or fear in his eyes as he looked across the ring, where Dos wore a look of overconfidence. The buzz in the gym was like the Colosseum in Rome. Two young gladiators preparing for battle.

East walked to the middle of the ring, still adjusting the mouthpiece comfortably in his mouth. They touched gloves, signaling the start of the fight. Before East could react, he was eating two quick jabs that bloodied his lip instantly. The overconfident smirk returned to Dos' face. East threw his first punch. Dos side-stepped it and threw another one. East slipped it and fired a punch of his own but missed badly. Dos chuckled. Showing his ring experience, he feinted with a jab then landing a hard-right hand that staggered East back into the ropes. With cat-like quickness Dos was right up on him. Left hook, right hook, smothering him with punches sending East into a protective shell. Purely off instinct, East threw a haymaker that connected to Dos' head, causing the smirk to disappear from his face. East shot a quick left hook that Dos dipped and returned a left hook to East's rib cage. He faked a right jab that made East throw up his guard to block his face, leaving himself open to a crushing kidney shot. Dos leveled him.

East let out a grunt. He was barely able to take the painful blow, staggering against the ropes unable to breath. Dos moved in for the kill, throwing a quick combo to the body and head dropping East to one knee gasping for air.

"No free lunch in here," Dos boasted as he swiped his nose with the glove.

Tez stepped between them but Ricardo intervened. "Don't stop it. Let them dawgs fight. You know the rules. Only the strong survive." He knew pressure would bust pipes. If East had any quit in him, it was bound to show itself inside that ring.

East sucked in air until he caught his breath. He looked over at Ricardo then up at Tez before rising to his feet.

"You good?" Tez whispered.

East nodded his head, dying for the chance to get back in the action. There was fire in his belly. As soon as Tez moved out the way, East shot a lazy jab that Dos slipped easily, then caught him with another combo. Two to the head, one to the body. This time East took it and came back with a vicious hook to the body and an uppercut that snapped Dos' head back, sitting him flat on his ass. The punch drew oohs and aahs from the other kids around the ring. No one had ever knocked Dos down before. Even Ricardo looked surprised.

Dos banged his gloves on the canvas in frustration, then jumped to his feet. Now, East was the one with the confident smirk on his face. The two circled and feinted at each other. This time with more respect for the other. Dos was the quicker of the two but East clearly hit harder. They stood in the middle of the ring going toe to toe, trading blows evenly until Ricardo called time. They still didn't stop. Neither would quit first, refusing to fold until Tez intervened, stepping between them and pulling them apart.

"That's enough," Ricardo commanded as he stepped inside the ring.

Both boys were exhausted, hunched over with their hands on their knees. Sweating and breathing heavily through their mouths.

"That was a good one. Y'all give it up for these two," Ricardo told the group around the ring. They all clapped. Ricardo was impressed by what he saw from the new kid. He already knew what his son was made of. Shit, his DNA flowed through him. But East had gained his respect. What the young kid lacked in skill, he more than made up for it with toughness and heart. A trait Ricardo was very fond of. "Lil' man got heart," he whispered to Tez.

"Crazy heart," Tez replied in his low raspy tone as they stood side by side.

"Yeah," Ricardo nodded his head. "I want to keep him close. So, I can keep my eye on him," Ricardo instructed.

"Definitely," Tez agreed. He was Ricardo's most trusted friend. His right hand man. They had been running together since they were kids. Ricardo felt confident with Tez by his side.

Dos stared across the ring at East. He would never admit it but that had been the toughest fight of his young life. East had gained his respect also. After catching his breath, he walked over with a smile identical to his father's and extended his hand. "That was some good work," he said with child-like enthusiasm.

East hadn't decided how he felt about Dos just yet, so he remained guarded and didn't shake his hand. He wasn't used to fighting someone than talking to them immediately after. It felt weird that Dos was standing in his face smiling, being friendly and wanting to talk. "Yeah, you too," he replied dryly.

"What's your name?" Dos questioned, curious to know more about the new face.

"East. Why?"

"Oh, your East," Dos said as the name rang a bell. "My dad told me about you."

"Who's your dad?" East asked, a bit confused.

Dos nodded towards Ricardo. "I'm Dos."

"Dos?"

"Yeah, like the number two in Spanish," he explained.

"Oh, so you're a Junior?" East asked.

Dos sucked his teeth. "Yeah but I hate being called that. Everybody calls me Dos," he made it clear. "Your dad and my dad are friends, right?"

"I guess they were," East said, looking over at Ricardo who was talking with Tez.

"Then how come I ain't never seen you around before?" Dos asked.

East shrugged his shoulders. "I ain't never seen you either."

"True," he agreed. "You're a little stiff. You gotta loosen up some. But you're cool," Dos joked.

East didn't reply. He still was deciding if he liked Dos or not.

"My dad about to take me to get some pizza, you wanna roll?" Dos offered.

"I guess," East answered and like that, their friendship had begun. East and Dos would become close. Had a thing or two gone differently in life, they might have remained that way.

* * *

Screw stood in the front of the apartments dribbling a basketball with his little cousin Que, while his twin sister, Samayah, sat on the stoop reading a book. "Man, it's boring out here," he huffed. "I'm bout to go to the park,"

"You better not. Mama said to stay right here, in front of the house," Samayah reminded him.

"Who is you, mama's watch dog or something. You need to mind ya business sometime," he snapped.

"I don't care what you say. You go and I'm telling," she promised never lifting her eyes from the book. "They be down there shooting at the park anyway. You need to stay your butt right here."

Screw sucked his teeth. She was always trying to get him in trouble. He stopped dribbling the ball and walked over to her. He slammed her book shut, looked her straight in the eyes and said, "Snitches get stitches." The look on his face was so serious, Samayah hesitated to reply.

Before she could, a black Mercedes pulling up in

front of their apartments drew their attention.

"Whose car is that?" Que asked in awe.

"I don't know but I'm bout to find out," Screw said, sprinting towards the sidewalk. When the car came to a complete stop, his mouth opened in shock when East emerged from the backseat. "Oh shit," he blurted out, giving his friend a pound.

East and Screw had been best friends since they first met. Whenever you saw one of them, the other was bound to be nearby.

"That's a MMMMMMaybach?" he asked, amazed by the luxury vehicle and mimicking the tag made famous by Miami rapper Rick Ross.

"Nah, just a Benz," East said less enthused but still with a smile on his face.

"Whose is it? Que asked, his little chubby face lighting up.

"Mine," Dos boasted.

Screw saw the unfamiliar face emerge from the backseat of the car. They locked eyes, glaring at each other. Screw didn't like new faces and He didn't like his position as East's best friend being threatened. He immediately felt like this new kid was trying to trespass on his territory, so he pressed the issue. "Who's the rich boy? And who he thinks he's lookin' at?"

"I'm looking at you. Why what's up?" Dos didn't back down from the challenge.

They started walking towards each other, until East stepped between them.

"Y'all chill out," he said, calmly pushing them apart easing the tension. "This is Dos. He cool," he introduced his new friend and assured his old one. "Dos, this my best friend Sameer, but we call him Screw. The little fat one, that's his cousin, Que," he said pointing.

"Who's that over there? She's kinda cute," Dos smiled and winked at Samayah, sitting on the stoop.

"What nigga! That's my sister," Screw barked.

"So what," Dos shrugged sarcastically.

"Dos!" Ricardo's voice boomed as he exited the car on the other side and rested his arms on the roof. He had heard enough of his son's cockiness and bravado. He didn't have to say anything else. Just by the way he'd called Dos' name and looked at him, he knew to knock it off.

At that moment, Angela walked out the front door of her apartment and on to the porch. Just in time to see Ricardo getting out the car. "Whose fine ass car is that?" she asked with a hint of her Dominican accent mixed with her Miami upbringing. She placed a hand over her large breast and took in the view, really referring to the handsome man getting out of it.

"I don't know," Samayah answered. "But East just got out that car and Screw..." she paused to correct herself, knowing her mother hated to him called by that name. "I mean Sameer was just trying to fight that other boy." She filled her mother in like she always did. Angela stood there with her arms folded, watching the boys but mainly Ricardo, until him and his son pulled off.

"Hey Ms. Ang," East smiled as he walked up. He jogged up the three steps of the stoop and planted a kiss on the side of her face.

"Hey baby," she smiled and hugged him. "Who was that?" she inquired about the mystery man.

"Oh, that was my friend Dos and his dad. They gave me a ride home from the gym."

Is there a Mrs. Dos' Dad in the picture? Angela thought to herself but knew better than to voice it. "What happened to your lip?" she voiced her concern, noticing the slight swelling and dried blood. "Sammi, go get him some ice."

Samayah jumped up quick more than willing to help but East stopped her.

"Nah, it's nothing, really, Ms. Ang," he dismissed, "It don't even hurt."

"Well your mother has to work late tonight, so she asked if you could eat dinner over here with us," Angela informed him.

"Ok," he answered. Ms. Ang cooked better than his mother, so he didn't mind at all.

"Ma, can we go to the park and play ball until dinner is done?" Screw asked, standing in place dribbling his ball.

"How you know he wanna to go?" Samayah sucked her teeth, frowning her face.

"How you know he don't?" Screw retorted. "Didn't I tell you earlier to mind ya business. You wanna go right East?" he looked at his friend trying to persuade him with his eyes.

"I'm with it," East replied.

"See." Screw bragged.

"Y'all can go," Angela said, "But, y'all better have y'all little asses back in this house before dinner is served. You hear me?"

"Yes ma'am." All three boys said in unison.

"Can I go?" Samayah asked.

"No. I need you to help me with dinner," Angela replied.

Samayah stood up, grabbed her book and stormed into the house. Her feelings clearly hurt. As soon as she got in the house, she plopped on the chair by the window. From there, she could see East, her brother and cousin walking to the park.

Angela stood in the kitchen and watched her daughter stare out the window. She knew Samayah had a little crush on East. She thought it was cute. "C'mere baby," she called to her as she sat down at the kitchen table. "Come sit next to me."

Samayah got up, walked over to her mother and sat down. Angela put her arm around her. "Lately, I've noticed the way you look at that boy, every time he comes around. You like him, don't you?"

"Who?" Samayah pretended not to know who her mother was talking about.

"Girl, don't play with me," Angela said. "You know exactly who I'm talking about. But since you need me to spell it out for you, I'm talking about East."

Samayah huffed and folded her arms, "No, I don't like him." She sucked her teeth.

"Good," Angela said knowing her daughter was lying. "Because you know, Tweet is like my sister. Which makes you and East like family."

Samayah remained quiet for a moment then looked up at her mother, "Family or like family mama? she asked for clarification. "Because you and Auntie Tweet ain't really sisters. So that means me and East ain't really family."

Angela couldn't help herself as she burst out laughing. "You always were my smartest child," she joked, pulling Samayah into her warm embrace. The two of them sharing a good laugh.

"I do like him tho, Mama," Samayah admitted in a low tone when the laughing stopped. "But it's like he doesn't even see me. He pays me no attention. He just wants to hang out with Sameer and Que all the time," she said with such sadness wrapped in her mother's arms.

Angela shook her head. Her baby girl had it bad. "Listen baby, for someone not to be able to see you or recognize your worth, they'd have to be blind." Angela lifted her daughters chin. "If so, be it East or some other boy, they aren't worth your time and effort. You're smart and you're beautiful and," she held her last word for a long time before finishing, "way too young to have boys on the brain. So, don't worry about that, pretty girl. When the time comes boys will be lining up at my front door for your attention. For now, just keep your head in them books and keep bringing home those good grades I love. Ok?"

"Yes, mama," she replied then rested her head on her mother. The two of them watched TV until dinner was ready.

CHAPTER SEVEN

Exhausted and happy to finally be off of work, Ebony exited the doors of the 24 hour Urgent Care clinic, to wait for a cab. When she stepped outside, she noticed a familiar face staring at her, and a nervous feeling crept into her stomach. Standing every inch of 6'2 beside a brand new 740ii BMW, smiling from ear to ear with pearly white teeth, deep dimples and beautiful chocolate skin was Lance. He approached with confidence in his stride.

"What's up, beautiful? Long time no see," he said entering her space bringing with him a manly scent of Calvin Klein cologne.

Ebony inhaled his scent. "Hey, Lance," she rolled her eyes. Most women couldn't help but lust over him. But Ebony was not most women. She never ran after men; they ran, fought, and even threatened to kill over her. Ebony knew how to use her beauty to her advantage. It was a powerful tool she used on men whenever she chose to. Lance was one of those men.

"Damn ma, a nigga been out here looking for you in the daytime with a flashlight. Where you been?" His eyes scanning her entire body. Ebony knew primal lust when she saw it. She had witnessed it in the eyes of men all her life. Lance wanted her, this she knew. His eyes told the story in detail.

"I been around," she said causally.

"I missed you," he admitted. "How you been doing?"

"Good, I guess. But I could always be doing better," she said.

"That's what I'm talkin' about. What can I do to help," Lance asked pulling her close, kissing her on the neck, first softly then more passionately, even after a long day at work, Ebony still smelled and tasted like French vanilla and honey,

"First, you can pump your brakes," she placed a hand on his stomach and pushed him away.

"My fault," he replied, easing back slightly.

"Then," she continued. "You can give me a ride

home, so I don't have to pay for a cab. Seeing how you came all the way up to my job and all," she sassed.

"No doubt," Lance answered smoothly like he had said the line a thousand times before. "I wanted to talk business with you anyway," he said licking his lips and rubbing his hands together.

Lance was still fine, Ebony had to admit to herself. They had fucked a few times over the years but nothing serious ever came from it. They did, however, have another type of partnership that Ebony wasn't interested in starting again.

Through her job as a medical assistant, Ebony had full access to doctor prescription pads. A very valuable commodity on the streets because they could be used to obtain dangerous medications. Lance was the go-to-man for the pills. Through Ebony he could get his hands on anything from antibaldness pills to Viagra. He moved discreetly, so she never worried about helping him or her business getting out in the street. It was different now. She wasn't trying to risk what she had for him. He was different. He appeared flashier than she remembered. Brand new whip, big chain, big watch.

"I already know what you want. And the answer is no. Hell no."

"Damn Eb, at least hear a nigga out, before you shoot me down," he charmed holding his hand over his chest. "I promise it will be worth it. I know you could use the extra money and shit."

"Oh, so now you trying to play me?" she sassed.

"C'mon, don't do me like that. You know I wouldn't do that. Shit, I'm just saying, we all could use some extras," he admitted.

"You don't look like you're hurting for nothing," she said, eyeing his new BMW as he held the door open for her.

Lance sighed. "Listen, I'm just a friend in need, who is willing to help the helper in return."

Ebony rolled her eyes and laughed. "Boy, stop. You know you can't G me."

"This ain't no G. For real, I got some new shit going," he swore.

I can tell, Ebony thought to herself but didn't share her thoughts. Choosing to play her cards close.

"So, are you gonna hear me out or what?" he begged.

"For as long as it takes to get me home," she said as she slid into the car. Lance smiled and closed the door.

As they drove through the streets heading for Ebony's apartment, Lance looked over at her. "A woman as beautiful as you, shouldn't be working all types of hours of the night. Having to pull doubles and shit like that. You should be able to do whatever, whenever your heart desires," he said. "Shit, I'm still trying to figure out why some nigga ain't wife you up yet."

She looked over at him and decided to entertain his conversation for a moment. "Why, that's what you trying to do, Lance?"

"Most definitely."

"Well, what if I ain't trying to be somebody's wifey?" Ebony smirked. "What if I'm trying to be somebody's wife?"

"I respect that," he asserted.

"No, you don't. Who you think you trying to fool," she laughed knowing he would say anything he could to get what he wanted,

"Check this out, you hungry? Cuz I know a nice little spot that stays open late," he offered smoothly.

"No. I just really want to get home, take a shower and get out of these clothes—," she paused, noticing a hint of mischief dancing in his eyes. "You're so damn nasty," she laughed.

"I'm saying. I could definitely help you out your clothes." He licked his full lips and eyed her lustfully.

Ebony laughed but inside she thought, *I could*

really use the release and this nigga do know how to work his tongue. Instead, she changed the subject. "So, what you really wanted to talk about, besides trying to get some pussy?" she stated boldly.

"Like I said, I got some real shit going on. Way bigger than before. Its more money in it for you too, if you can help me out," he said like a seasoned pitch man. "I need to get my hands on this shit called Tramadol," he stumbled to pronounce the word. "It's a synthetic opioid."

"Tramadol. I know what it is," Ebony stated.

"Yeah, well them white folks out in Adventura and Pembroke Pines going crazy over the shit. And I need to get my hands on some Promethazine with Codeine, ASAP," he pressed.

"I'on know Lance. That's some heavy shit you're asking for. Too risky for me to be doing. I gotta son to think about—"

"Exactly," he cut her off. "Think about your son. He's getting big as a muthafucka. Jordans and all that fly shit I know he like, it ain't cheap. You always been a go getter, taking care of him on your own. I'm just trying to help. We did it before."

"Yeah but this is different. Way different," she explained.

"All you gotta do is get me the shit or the scripts

to get them. I'll take care of everything else," he implored.

The car got silent as they pulled in front of her apartment.

"Just think about it. You don't have to give me an answer right now but I'm gonna need one soon," he explained.

"I'll think about it," she said to which he smiled because it wasn't a no. He really needed her to come through.

Lance looked towards her apartment, seeing all the lights were off, he asked, "Is your son sleep?"

"He's not home. He's staying the night over at Ang's," she said looking towards the door of her friend's apartment, who only stayed across the courtyard from her.

"So, you gonna let a nigga come in or what?" he flirted.

"I don't know, Lance. Maybe some other time," she forced herself to say, really wanting to. She hadn't had some dick in a while, and *it wasn't like he was new*, she told herself.

Saying nothing, Lance moved closer and kissed her. Ebony slowly rubbed her hand on his leg. Lance could already feel his dick getting hard in his pants. He reached over, placing his hand on the inside of her thigh and finessed his hand up her leg. Ebony went with it and didn't stop him as he pulled at the tie on her scrubs. He continued to kiss her then slipped his hand inside her pants, rubbing her through the silk panties she wore underneath.

"I just want to taste you," he pleaded as his dick continued to swell.

Ebony's clit was pulsating. The puddle forming in her panties had her ready to submit to his request. She wanted to lead him inside her apartment and sit her juicy pussy on his face. Ebony sat her seat back and held her breath as he moved her panties to the side. She released a passionate moan when she felt his fingers enter her. The car was quiet. The only sound was her wetness as he moved his fingers in and out of her. With her eyes closed and her head resting on the headrest, she softly bit down on her lip and moaned. Lance was making her drip with ecstasy. Ebony opened her eyes and noticed the bulge in his pants. She smiled again, her body surging with desire. Lance eyes were filled with sexual hunger. He craved her. Ebony turned her hips towards him, to make it easier for him to reach her G-spot. Lance couldn't control himself. All he could think about was digging deep inside of her, deeper than anyone had ever gone before.

Ebony moaned as he began to move his fingers faster. "Oh," she cried out.

"Give me that shit ma. Cum all over my fingers," Lance commanded and soon after Ebony's body surrendered to his demands.

Ebony's chest heaved up and down. She looked over at Lance and said, "C'mon."

He cut the car off, got out and followed her to the door. Once inside, he pressed her against the door and kissed her passionately.

"In my room," she said between kisses.

Lance cut her off with another kiss. "I want you right here, right now." He slid his hand inside her panties again. He massaged her clit then slipped his fingers into her wet pussy as he licked her neck. "Damn ma, that pussy so wet." He unbuttoned his pants.

Ebony gyrated on his fingers. Grabbing the back of his head as they kissed again. "Oh, that feels so good," she moaned.

They were suddenly startled, hearing movement behind them, Ebony quickly turned to see East standing in the hallway. Still half sleep, his head cocked to the side like a confused puppy trying to understand what he was seeing.

"Ma, you alright?" he asked.

Ebony's heart sunk to her stomach. She felt so embarrassed quickly pushing Lance away. "East what are you doing here? I thought you were staying at Angela's. You scarred me," her heart was pounding as she walked over to him, hugging him tightly.

"I wanted to sleep in my own bed," he answered.

"Yes, baby. I'm fine," she assured him. Ebony looked back at Lance and swore she could see him blushing through his dark skin as he fixed his clothes. His face was filled with awkwardness and he was at a loss for words. "You remember my friend Lance. He gave me a ride home from work. He just came in to make sure I was okay."

"Yeah, well she okay. You can leave now," East asserted, his shoulder hunched in anger. He could feel his heart swell in his chest. He balled his fist tight, scowling at Lance. He knew right then that he didn't like the nigga.

"He was just leaving, baby," Ebony motioned with her eyes to Lance, who tried to hide the smirk on his face. *Lil' nigga ain't playing bout his mother*, he laughed to himself. He said his goodnights then exited the apartment as smooth as he entered. "Don't forget about what we talked about," he reminded Ebony. "Call me," he called out while walking down the steps of the apartment.

Ebony locked the door behind him then turned back to East. He had hurt and anger in his eyes. She felt horrible. "I'm sorry you had to see that," she apologized not knowing what else to say.

East didn't respond. He just turned around, walked to his room and closed the door.

"East," she called out to him. Ebony sighed as she lingered in his doorway, tears of shame pooling in her eyes. She prided herself on being discreet in her dealings with men. She made sure East never witnessed different men coming and going or sneaking in and out of their apartment. She considered entering his room and talking to him but decided against it. She felt deflated as she turned and walked to her room.

* * *

"Girl, he did what?" Angela shouted on the other end of the phone, unable to contain her laughter.

"Yes, girl! Had his fist balled up and everything," Ebony explained from the comfort of her couch as she talked to her best friend the next morning.

"That East is gonna be hell when he gets older. That's one helluva young man you're raising, Tweet," Angela said.

"Who you telling Ang? I already know. My baby just gotta learn to control his temper."

Ebony had filled her friend in on the events of the past night, sparing her the details about Lance wanting her to help him get illegal drugs. She hadn't made up her mind yet, but she was strongly considering it.

"Maybe boxing will help. It teaches discipline," Angela expressed.

"Yeah, I guess you're right."

"Where's he at now?" Ang asked.

"At the gym again, why?"

"I just wanted to make sure he wasn't around you, cuz' I got some tea for you," Ang said, her voice lowering into a whisper.

"What is it?' Ebony sat up on the couch.

"Girl, my poor baby got a crush on East. And she got it bad too. I'm talkin' like Usher," Ang explained.

"Samayah?"

"Who else?" Ang cracked.

"Aww, my poor baby," Ebony said.

"I know, right?" Angela exhaled deeply. "Can't say I blame her though. East is a little cutie," Ang said.

"Watch ya mouth. That's my baby you talkin' bout," Ebony jokingly warned her friend.

"Girl stop it! You know that boy is fine as hell. Everybody knows it. Looking like his got damn daddy," Angela declared. "But I told Samayah, she too young to have boys on the brain. But between me and you, I was happy to know my baby got good taste." Both women laughed. "But back to you, puta."

"What?" Ebony asked like she didn't know where her friend was about to go.

"Are you gonna see Lance again?" Angela's voice lowering to a whisper as she filled with excitement and anticipation.

"I...I don't know, girl," Ebony was unsure. Her body wanted to but after what had happened with East, she didn't know if it was worth the trouble.

"What you mean, you don't know? When was the last time you got some dick? You better let that man knock the dust off that pussy," she joked, mimicking Chris Tucker in Friday.

"Whatever," Ebony laughed. "First of all, I don't need nobody to knock the dust off nothing over here. Speak for yourself."

"Hmph. Don't worry about me. I don't need no nigga for nothing. I'm doing just fine. My toys keep me satisfied and sucka free," Angela snapped back.

"Mhm. That's why you got carpel tunnel now."

"Fuck you," Ang shot back as both women broke out into laughter.

"Ma..."

"Ma, I'm hungry..."

Ebony could hear the voices of Angela's twin's coming through the phone. She knew that was her friend's que.

"Girl, these kids just walked in and their working my last nerve already," Angela huffed. "Let me get up and fix them something to eat before I catch a DFCS case."

"Tell my babies Auntie said hey," Ebony cooed. "I'll call you later on."

Ebony relaxed back into the comfortable cushions of her sofa and laughed to herself. Angela was right, it had been a while since she had some *good* dick. "Maybe I should give Lance a call," she mumbled under her breath. "His stroke game ain't all that, but that nigga know he can eat some pussy." She smiled at the recollection. She also thought about his proposal. *I could use the extra money around here.* She got quiet as she contemplated. *It would be good to be able to spend more time with East too.* She was killing herself with extra shifts just to make ends meet. She was also spending less time with the one person she loved the most in the world. East was growing up so fast, soon he wouldn't even want to spend as much time with her. As a mother, Ebony wanted to take advantage while she still could. "I'll call Lance later. Let me get up and clean this house," she huffed.

About an hour after cleaning the entire apartment, Ebony found herself sitting on the edge of the tub, watching the water run. Stevie Wonder's *These Three Words* playing in the background. A lone tear resting in the corner of her eye, waiting to fall at any second. She felt like the weight of the world had suddenly fallen upon her, causing the tear she tried to suppress, to roll down her cheek. It was followed by another and another. She didn't know why or where these feelings had come from. One minute she was fine and the next, she felt the walls closing in. The storm of sadness had hit so suddenly, out of nowhere and now she couldn't stop crying. This was her new normal. All kinds of thoughts were swirling in her mind as she sobbed painfully. There was so much hurt bottled up inside her. Family secrets. Abandonment. Motherhood. She dealt with it all bravely in front of the eyes of the world but behind closed doors, Ebony sometimes wondered how she hadn't put a bullet through her head yet. She turned off the water and stood in front of the mirror. Looking at herself, all she felt was disappointment. *She should've been better. She should've done better. She should've known better,* her parents' words replayed in her mind after they disowned her for shaming the family's good name by becoming pregnant as a teenager. It was always her fault, let them tell it. But that was far from the truth.

"The family's good name. Some good name," she huffed.

Everything seemed perfect in the James household from the outside looking in, but Ebony was on the inside and knew better. Her family was far from picture perfect. For her, it was a living hell growing up under that roof. Ebony's oldest brother had began molesting her as soon as she developed breast. It started in middle school. He would sneak into her room every night and rape her. She would cry and he would promise to never do it again, only to return the next night. She suffered in silence for years.

Until she met a Derek Eastwood that one summer. Ebony fell head over heels in love with him. She saw him as her a way to escape from what was happening in her home and she tried to spend every waking moment with him. Anything to be out of her house. Derek was the man she wanted to run away with. She couldn't bring herself to tell her parents what her brother was doing to her. It would break their heart. Destroy their family. Her brother was the apple of her father's eye. A high school football star just like he once was. Ebony loved her father so much. She couldn't stomach the thought of telling him the truth. She knew it would kill him. So, she clung to Derek and spent last time with the family. Her parents complained but she ignored them. It was long before Derek became the first man, she had sex with willing. When she found out she was pregnant she was overjoyed. But that happiness quickly disappeared when Derek abruptly did. Ebony still found a silver lining in her heartbreak. Once the family found out she was pregnant, the rapes stopped. Her brother just stopped. When her parents tried to convince her to get an abortion, she refused. Not only because she was already attached to the new life growing in her stomach, but also because the baby was her shield. Her only protection and line of defense from her brother's twisted love. East saved her. He saved her then and he saved her now. Just the fact that he existed in the whole thing and loved her the way he did, let Ebony know that there was light at the end of her depression.

She lifted the glass of water off the sink and held a Xanax in the palm of the other. She placed the pill in her mouth and quickly washed it down with the water. She couldn't wait for the pill to kick in. She strolled over to the tub and stepped inside, dipping her body in to the soothing hot water. She rested her head against a rolled-up towel, closed her eyes and waited for the calming feeling to take over her body.

PART II: TRAUMA

CHAPTER EIGHT: THREE YEARS LATER

Ricardo rose from the bed and stepped over to the window. His dream still playing vividly in his mind. It was the one he had most nights. Derek's murder three years ago. Navarro had ordered the hit after suspecting Derek of cooperating with the Feds. He tasked Ricardo with carrying it out. There was nothing he could've done to stop it. Had he tried he would've looked like he was protecting a snitch. It would have possibly meant his death as well. *And where would that have left Dos?* Alone in the world, without a dad. Ricardo would never let that happen.

Killing Derek had also proven to be lucrative. It had earned him favor with the cartel and Navarro. He was now making more money than he ever had.

Ricardo parted the curtains in his room and stared down at Dos, who was swimming laps in the pool. Something he did every morning. Ricardo swelled with pride. Dos was the heir to his throne. A new, improved version of himself. All his good, none of his flaws. All he was building. Ricardo was grooming Dos to be king of someday.

Lauryn eased up behind him and slithered her arms around his waist. "You're up early," she said.

"Couldn't sleep."

"Maybe because you're always so tense," she rubbed the back of his neck then moved her hands to his shoulders and massaged. "You need to learn how to relax."

"Easier said than done," he explained.

Lauryn understood the life. That's what made her the perfect woman for him. She was a hustler's wife that had been raised by a hustler, around hustlers her whole life. "No, it's not. You make it harder than it has to be," she explained. When he turned to face her, she kissed him on the lips. "Let me help you get your day started right," she purred seductively, opening her robe exposing her perfect body. She lowered to her knees in front of him.

Ricardo stopped her, pulling her back to her feet. "Maybe another other time," he rejected. "I have to get dressed but you can go start breakfast," he said, kissing her forehead and walking passed her into the closet.

Lauryn stood frozen in the middle of the room. Rejection coursed through her body. Lately, it had become the norm. Ricardo's lack of affection and attention. The more his business grew, the less time they spent together. She spent most of her days surrounded by guards and henchmen, locked away in their massive estate. She felt like a prisoner in her own home. Nothing more than Ricardo's beautiful trophy. There to be seen and not heard. Her only escape was when she went shopping. Something she did a lot of. Lauryn tied her silk robe closed before heading downstairs to the kitchen.

Dos came up on the edge of the pool, panting as he finished his early morning workout. His pulse was racing, and he could feel the blood pumping through his heart. He was ready for the day. The warm Miami sun hit his face as he eased out of the water and grabbed a towel. Wiping his face first then wrapping it around his waist, low enough to show off the V-cuts in his lower abdomen. Now 18, Dos had grown into a handsome young man. He was a magnet for attention; mostly from girls who couldn't resist his mixture of good looks, charm and swagger. He had low, curly hair, soft brown skin and a body like a Greek God from years of training as a boxer.

Lauryn sipped her mimosa while watching Dos through the floor to ceiling windows in the kitchen. He walked into the kitchen as she was placing a freshly sliced bowl of fruit on the island. "Good morning," she greeted.

"What's up," he replied, reaching for a piece of fruit.

Lauryn knocked his hand away. "Wash your hands first," she scolded. "And put a shirt on."

Dos ignored her and took a piece out the bowl anyway. He walked over to the fridge and removed a bottle of water. "What's for breakfast?" he asked before gulping down the water and tossing the empty bottle on the counter.

"You too, geez" she huffed as she stood over the stove. "You sound like your father. Is that all I'm good for around here?" she complained, shaking her head.

Dos shrugged his shoulders as he eyed her up and down. "I don't know. You are the lady of the house, right?" he asked.

"Yeah, but I'm not a maid," Lauryn exhaled as she

picked the empty bottle of water off the counter. She waved it at him, perfect example of what she meant, then tossed it into the garbage.

"Yeah, but you sure 'nuff got it made," he reminded her before grabbing another piece of fruit and walking out the kitchen.

"Whatever," Lauryn uttered, giving a half-hearted smirk at his comment. Dos was full of confidence. That type of bravado came with youth, but it bordered on arrogance sometimes.

"Whatever, what?" Ricardo asked as he entered the kitchen, just a tad too late to hear what had been said.

"Nothing." Lauryn answered and turned back towards to stove. "Breakfast is almost done," she explained.

"Make it for one," Ricardo declared as he walked over to the fridge and snatched a water bottle out. "I have to go."

Lauryn rolled her eyes. "I'm tired of being cooped up in this house."

Ricardo paused and looked around at the massive kitchen of his elegant estate that sat on the water. "You're far from cooped up, baby," he said as he wrapped his arms around her and pulled her to him. "You're just pouting. How bout you go shopping today? Buy yourself some new things, to add to all the new things you got already," he laughed. "Get out the house for a little while," he suggested. That was music to her ears until he said, "I'll have a few of the guys take you."

Lauryn exhaled deeply and slumped her shoulders. "Why does your paid robots have to go everywhere with me? Why can't I go alone or with one of my friends?" she complained.

"I told you before, it's for your own safety. And for my own peace of mind," he said softly.

She sighed. "I guess. Do I really have a choice?" she gripped.

"Of course, you do," Ricardo said smoothly, kissing her on the forehead. "Two choices. Take it or leave it." Then he walked out the kitchen, concluding their conversation on his terms.

CHAPTER NINE

East stood in front of the door of his apartment, talking to Screw and Que. He was growing up fast. Not only in height, standing 6'2" with a slim, muscular, athletic body, but in knowledge as well. He thirsted for it. The need to know more was what drove him. Every chance he got, he would head to the gym to train with Dos but mostly to soak up game from Ricardo and Tez. They had become his mentors, like the fathers that he needed in his life. He was learning the world around him through them. While learning their different approaches to life by their styles of training. Ricardo's style was brazening, tough and in your face. He had a very hardnose approach. There was a lot of yelling and cursing when he was training you. Never mean spirited but it served its purpose.

Tez's on the other hand, had a more laid back temperament that appealed to East. With him, East's brain always got more of a workout then his body did. They would have long conversations about important things in life. Tez would school him through boxing lessons, while passing down jewels and codes of the street. East was receiving a dual education like none other. When both men spoke, he absorbed everything with a grasp that exceeded his age.

East had become like a second son to Ricardo. But with Tez, it was deeper. East was the son he never even knew he wanted. There was just something about East that Tez's callous demeanor softened to. He was smart for his age, very attentive but most importantly, East was fearless. Tez knew he was a special breed, rather East knew it yet or not.

"Yo, we need to rob that nigga that be coming through here to check your mom," Sameer suggested. "The nigga with the BMW."

"Who Lance?" East asked, nonchalantly as if he wasn't taking his friend seriously.

"Yeah, that nigga's getting' money," Sameer's eyes lit up.

"You trippin'," East replied.

Although East and Sameer were best of friends, the two young men were nothing alike. East was a thinker, who meticulously plotted out everything he did. He never went into any situation without analyzing every aspect of it first. He was quiet, observing and humble, with a strong ambition to succeed. He gave respect to those who deserved it, and respect was what he got in return.

"Man, fuck that nigga! Que, wit it. Right?"

"Yeah," Que said backing his cousin's play.

Sameer was the total opposite of East. He was a hot head, who solved all his problems with violence. Screw didn't want people to respect him. He wanted them to fear him. The word in the neighborhood was that he was crazy and dangerous. The only people Sameer had love for was those he considered family. The only people he trusted was East and his little cousin, Que. At 16, he was a year younger than East and an inch shorter, but he had already committed his share of crimes. And he knew East and Que would never say a word about them to anyone.

"Even though I wouldn't lose no sleep if it happened. Y'all can't be the ones to rob the nigga Lance," East shook his head, like he hated having to explain what seemed so obvious to him.

"Why not," Sameer asked, unruliness in his eyes.

""Think about it. That shit could fall back on my mother. What if he thinks she set him up or something? It ain't worth it."

Sameer went quiet. He definitely didn't want that. He loved Ms. Ebony. She was family. Although he hated to admit it, East had a point. Either way, he was gonna figure out a way to make some money. "Still, we need to be getting to this money".

"What's stopping you," East challenged.

"You,.right now. You trying to be boxing champ of the whole world and shit." Sameer joked. "You think you Floyd Mayweather nigga?" he teased, throwing playful punches into East's chest. They all laughed.

"You funny," East said as they all laughed.

"There goes ya boy," Que interrupted, seeing a tinted, black Ford F-150 drive up and park in front of the apartments.

Dos sat behind the wheel, waiting for East. He never bothered to get out. He didn't have time to chill and talk. Instead, he rolled the window down and nodded, "What up?" to Sameer and Que.

"What up," Both replied. Although, they were friendly with Dos, they weren't exactly friends. The only thing they all had in common was East.

"That's the nigga we need to get," Sameer said with a smirk. "Bitch ass nigga," he uttered under his breath.

"You still on that shit? You need to relax. That's my nigga," East explained.

"He's your nigga, not mine," Sameer reminded him than laughed.

East just shook his head. He knew Sameer was just talking shit, but it wasn't cool. "I'll be back later," he said, slapping five with his friends before leaving them behind.

"I don't know why East keeps hanging with that nigga," Sameer said, watching his friend walk towards the truck.

"He ain't that bad. You just don't like him," Que laughed as they watched the truck pull away.

"Man, take your lil' fat ass in the house," Sameer snapped. "I'm out. If my mother ask's you didn't see me," he instructed then he walked the opposite way.

"What's up, bro?" Dos asked, as East settled into the truck. They gave each other a pound, then relaxed. "I need you to take a ride with me somewhere. It's important."

"What you up to now?" East asked. "I thought we was going to the gym."

"Don't start that shit today, East. I just need you

to ride with me. Hold me down,"

"Hold you down?" East looked at him suspiciously. "Oh, I know you on some bullshit for now." He had gotten used to Dos and his antics.

Dos laughed.

Twenty minutes later, they pulled up and parked in front of a Blue's Barber Shop in Opa-Locka.

"Yo, what are we doing over here?" East asked, scanning his eyes back and forth, up and down the block. He was on alert. "I know you ain't gettin your hair cut. So, what's up?"

"Chill, we good. I just had to come check my man Kev, real quick," Dos explained. He reached behind East's seat and grabbed a black bookbag. "Like I said I just need you to hold me down." He opened the bag, removed a Glock 9mm and slipped it in his waistband.

"I hope you got one in there for me," East said.

"Nah, it ain't like that. C'mon," Dos said with a smile.

"I can't tell," East declared.

They both got out of the car and walked inside. The shop was crowded with everyday customers. Men that sat around talking about sports, politics and lying on their dicks. Not to mention the older men that sat around and reminisced about their glory days. Dos walked through the crowd shaking hands and speaking, while East remained silent and on point. Only offering an occasional head nod. After making their way to the back, they went up a flight of stairs and stopped at a black door. Dos knocked a few times, until a voice answered on the other side.

"Come in."

Dos pushed open the door and he and East entered the room, closing the door behind them. A man in his early twenties with brown skin and long dreadlocks was sitting on a sofa in front of a TV, smoking weed.

"My nigga Dos," he stood to greet him.

"Kev, what up," Dos replied dapping him up. "This my bro, East."

East nodded and Kev did in return.

Kev was a young drug dealer on the come up. He was also a free agent. He had once worked for his older brother, Blue, that ran a small organization, supplying a few small-time neighborhood drug dealers. But Blue, along with most of his crew had recently caught a fed case and were down. Now, Kev was looking to fill those shoes and step up in his brother's absence.

"Have a seat," Kev said, pointing the remote at the TV and turning it off. "You smoke?' he offered.

Both declined. Dos and East took a seat on the smaller sofa directly across from Kev.

"I appreciate you looking out the way you did, last time," Kev said. "Shit, really got me back on my feet."

"You know it's all love, my nigga. You got the bread?" Dos responded looking to move things along quicker.

"Right here." Kev looked at them, then reached into the cushions of the couch.

Dos immediately reached for the gun on his waist.

Kev's eyes lit up. "Yo, be easy, my nigga. I ain't on it like that." He pulled a knot of money from out the couch. He handed it over to Dos, who then removed an 8-ball of coke from the bookbag and tossed it to him. "This the same shit as before?" Kev examined the product with excitement in his eyes.

"Same shit," Dos assured as he placed the money inside the bag and zipped it closed.

"Cool," Kev said as he rose to his feet. Dos and East did the same.

"When you looking to get more?" Dos asked.

Kev thought about it for a second. "I'll call you next week."

"That's what's up. Let's make it more beneficial

for the both of us, next time. Know what I'm saying," Dos explained smoothly, indicating he wasn't for the nickel and dime shit Kev was copping. He didn't want to waste his time for scraps. He shook Kev's hand then walked out.

After Dos and East had left the room, Kev sat back down on the sofa and reached for the remote to turn the TV back on.

Dos and East exited the barbershop and got back in the truck. As they pulled away from the shop, East sat back shaking his head.

"What's wrong East? Spit it out," Dos said, seeing the look on his face.

"Yo, what the fuck was that back there? Your Pops know you doing that?"

"Nah. And he ain't gonna find out, if you don't say shit," Dos snapped as he weaved through traffic.

"You know that's the last thing you gotta worry about. But you trippin'," East asserted.

"Let me ask you something," Dos' tone got serious. "What you think my Pops really do? You think we live the way we do, and he drives those cars, cause of boxing? Or the gym?" Dos laughed. "You can't be that naive, my nigga."

"I look stupid to you?" East shot back. "I know what your Pops does. I also know he's gonna kill you when he finds out what you're doing. Where you get that shit from anyway?" East asked referring to the coke Dos had sold to Kev.

"Where you think?" Dos stated boldly, looking over at East and raising his eyebrows. The car got quiet as they stared at each other.

"I know you ain't stealing from your Pops," East said with a serious tone and face to match. Dos' silence confirmed his guilt. "Nah, you can't be doing that. You ain't that stupid," he huffed. "You ain't got the sense God gave you," East shook his head. "He gonna kill you and that nigga Kev back there when he finds out."

"He ain't gonna find out!" Dos swore.

"It ain't cool to bite the hand that feeds you. You should remember that." East said.

"Speaking of, I'm hungry. How bout you? I ain't eat all day," Dos changed the subject. "Let's go eat. It's on me," he smirked, patting the bookbag full of cash.

A few minutes later the two of them sat across from one another inside IHOP, waiting for their order to be taken. Dos sat his menu down and picked back up on their earlier conversation. "I got Mario down too," he confessed. Knowing East knew what he was talking about. "He don't know where I'm getting it from tho."

East leaned back in his seat and shook his head. "No disrespect, but your cousin Rio is a fuck up. I can't believe you're fuckin' with him. That nigga gonna get you and him, locked up or killed. Plus, I don't trust his ass. His eyes always be looking all beady and shit."

"I trust him. He's my cousin," Dos said.

"Good luck with that," East shrugged.

"It would've been me and you, bro but you—"

"Nah, I'm good on that," East interrupted him.

"See. That's what I'm talking about. That's exactly why I put Rio down instead," he passionately replied. "It's like you too cool for school or some shit."

"It ain't that. You just too reckless for me," East explained. He knew his time would come to get in the game but like everything else he did, he was being strategic. Nobody was going to push him.

"I could give you some to move," Dos offered. "It's J's all around your projects. You, Screw and Que could—"

At that moment the waitress arrived at their table to take their order. "Hey, what can I get y'all?" she asked.

They both looked up and were pleasantly surprised for different reasons. Dos thought the girl standing in front of him was beautiful. East recognized her.

"Jasmine?"

"Hey, East. What's up?" she replied cheerfully with a strong New York accent.

"Damn, I haven't seen you since middle school. I didn't know you worked here," he said.

"Definitely, been a minute," she replied with a smile.

"I see I'm gonna have to start coming here more often," Dos interrupted to flirt. Jasmine was gorgeous. She had a flawless mocha skin tone with full pouty lips and deep dish dimples. Her ass still looked round and curvy despite the loose-fitting uniform she wore. Dos had to have her.

She smiled hard. "Can I take your order?"

"Yeah and my phone number," Dos offered as she blushed again.

She took their orders then disappeared from the table. The whole time East felt like a third wheel in their energy. While Dos couldn't stop staring at her ass as she walked away.

"You know her?" he whispered. "You fucked her? Man, I don't even care if you fucked her, but did you fuck that bitch?" he inquired, secretly hoping East said no.

"Nah, it ain't like that. I went to middle school

with her. Tell you the truth, I didn't know she was back in town. Last I heard, her and her family moved back to New York or some shit," East explained.

"Put me on, nigga," Dos pleaded.

East chuckled. "Put yourself on," he laughed then sipped his orange juice.

Dos smirked. He got up and walked across the restaurant towards Jasmine, who was taking another table's order. When she turned around, she was surprised by Dos' standing in her way.

"Is everything okay?" she asked a bit startled by his presence.

"You should let me take you out," Dos proclaimed with a handsome smile.

"And why should I do that?" she sassed, rolled her eyes and walked around him.

Dos followed behind her. "Damn ma, what happened to all the smiles you was giving over there at my table?"

"That's part of my job. It's called customer service," she countered.

"C'mon, let me take you out?" he tried turning on the charm.

"Why would you wanna do that?"

"Why wouldn't I?" he countered.

"Dos, please," she replied and rolled her eyes

again.

"Oh, so you know who I am."

"Who don't know you...with your hoe ass," Jasmine stated and walked into the kitchen. Dos followed. "What are you doing?" she screamed, looking around in panic and laughing nervously at his persistence. "You can't be in here."

"First of all, I go wherever I want to go. Secondly, I ain't a hoe," he said seriously.

"Excuse me, young man. You can not be in here, " the manager walked in and said.

Dos ignored her. "You gonna let me take you out?" he asked Jasmine.

"Young man!" the manager said again this time more aggressively.

"C'mon, at least give me your number."

"Jasmine, please let your friend know that if he doesn't leave now. I will call the police," the manager scolded.

"C'mon, Dos, go, before you go to jail," Jasmine pleaded with him.

"Then take me to jail," he said putting out both hands waiting for his wrist to be cuffed. "Cuz I'm not leaving until you give me your number, or the police come," he poked out his lips and pouted like a little child.

Jasmine giggled. She knew what kind of guy Dos was rumored to be, but she had to admit, *he was sexy as hell.* Word around town was his dick game was crazy too. "Ok, give me your phone," she requested unable to contain her smile.

Dos handed it to her. Jasmine dialed her number into it and pressed send. Her phone rang in her pocket then she handed his phone back to him.

"Now we got each other," she said.

"Nah, I got you," he said. "I'ma call you later."

"Ok. Now go, before you go to jail or get me fired," she said beaming from ear to ear as she pushed him out the kitchen.

CHAPTER TEN

Sameer picked the wrong day for a joyride. Now there were three cop cars already on his tail. He whipped around a corner, nearly tipping the car over in the process then mashed the pedal to the floor. His heart was pounding with adrenaline as he pushed the engine of the stolen Audi A7 to its limit. *If I could make it back to the projects, I can lose them,* he thought to himself. He wasn't trying to go to jail today. More police cars lights flashed in the rearview as he flew through the streets of Miami lawlessly, playing a dangerous game of cat and mouse. His long, curly hair blowing wildly in the wind as he zipped in and out of traffic, hitting speeds of over 100mph. He quickly turned down another block, leaving a long skid mark behind him.

"Fuck y'all niggas," he shouted, sticking his middle finger out the sunroof and laughing. With the project up ahead, he was almost home free. Suddenly a kid ran out in the middle of the street to pick up his football. Screw swerved to avoid him, nearly missing the kid but losing control in the process. The car spun. The sound of his tires screeching to a stop howled through the air as the Audi did a complete 360 degree turn and hopped the curb.

Screw leaped from the car and took out on foot into the projects. He ran through some clothes hanging outside on a clothesline then dipped around the corner of an apartment. He didn't make it far before he heard a cop yell "Freeze!" Screw didn't listen. He kept running, that's when he heard the gun shot.

* * *

When East and Dos arrived back at Pork and Beans, there were flashing red lights and police cars everywhere. *A normal occurrence*, East thought as Dos pulled the F150 up to the curb and parked.

"Thanks for rollin' wit' me today bro," Dos said. "Think about what I said. The offer still stands. If you want in, all you gotta do is say the word. You my family too," he promised. Dos reached in the bag and pulled out some of the money he had made with Kev. "Here, this yours."

"For what?"

"For holding me down today," Dos said excitedly.

"That's yours bro. I was just doing what I was supposed to do. Like you said, we family. And family looks out for each other," East explained. "Just think about what I said," he reminded Dos. "It's a right way to do everything. Even the wrong thing." Then he dapped Dos up and got out the car.

Dos watched East walk away. *He had a point*, he thought to himself as he sat there a moment before pulling off. In his heart, Dos knew stealing drugs from his father was wrong. But the wad of money in his hand and bookbag made it make sense in his mind. At least for the time being. "I gotta figure out another way but until then I'm getting this money. I don't care what East talkin' bout. That nigga trippin'," he declared before putting the cash back in the bookbag and pulling off.

East bent the corner and noticed the crowd in the courtyard, growing in front of Ms. Ang's door. There was a buzz in the air. Then he saw his mother, holding her best friend as she cried hysterically at the top of the stoop. Samayah and Que at their sides, both looked in shock. His heart sank when he didn't see Sameer at Ms. Ang's side. Something inside told him, her tears were for him. Call it intuition or instincts but East knew something. He made a beeline for the stoop.

"Ma, what's going on?" he asked in a feverish pitch as he made it over to them. "What's wrong with Ms. Ang?" he repeated himself quickly, more aggressively when his mother didn't answer fast enough. "Ma, what's wrong with Ms. Ang? Why is she crying? Samayah, why are all these police out here? Que, why everybody standing around what happened?" he rambled off a series of question, giving no one the space between them to answer. He could feel his heart pounding in his chest. A nervous tension choked the air and East felt like he was breathing it in to his lungs. A knot swelled in his throat. He bit down on his lip, fighting back tears as he asked his next question, "Where's Screw at?"

Ms. Ang's cries grew louder, hearing that name. That God forsaking name. The name the streets called her son by. The name she hated so much. She buried her face into Ebony's embrace unable to answer.

East stood silently, a serious look on his face as he nervously waited for an answer.

"Sameer's been arrested, East," Ebony informed her son. "He stole a car today and took the cops on a high-speed chase," she shook her head. "He's in the back of that police car, right there," she pointed.

East's face lowered in sadness. It was like he had just received the worst news of his life. Without hesitation, he turned and walked over to the police car where Sameer sat handcuffed in the back When he saw East walking towards him, he cracked a smile.

"What's up bro," he said through the glass, then paused and put his head down. When their eyes met again, his were watery but he didn't let a tear fall. "Promise me you're gonna look out for my mom and my sister while I'm gone."

"Don't worry, I'm got them," East said seriously. "You just stay out of trouble while you're gone. And watch your back. I heard them niggas in juvenile hall is wild."

"Don't worry about me. I can hold my own," he said confidently.

East touched the window with his fist like the was fist bumping Sameer, then the cop car pulled off. Sameer looked back as his best friend and the projects grew further and further away. When he was certain East could no longer see him, he let the tears in his eyes roll down his face and cried silently.

Back in front of Ms. Ang's apartment, Samayah was sitting alone on the stoop with her head down crying. East walked over and took a seat next to her. Samayah looked up at him with her pretty face and watery amber eyes and said, "I can't take this anymore. Somebody's always getting shot or going to jail around her. I hate living here." Tears fell down her face.

East reached out and gave her a warm hug. "It's gonna be alright," he said.

"It's gonna be so different without Sameer around now. I feel like half of me is missing already," she cried.

"I know, but you got me," East said sincerely as he released her from his embrace. He held her hand.

"I know," Samayah said half-heartedly, because she wished his words were true. But *you ain't checking for me like that*, she told herself. "I'm going away for school next year," she revealed. "FAMU, Florida State, somewhere."

"Huh?" he asked in surprise. "I thought you were staying close and going to U of M?"

"Not anymore," she declared. "I haven't decided which school yet but I'm not staying around here," she said, wiping her tears.

"You're really serious about leaving, huh?"

"Yes, East. It's the only way I can get away from this place and –." She really wanted to say him but stopped herself.

They sat in silence for a moment, just staring out at the projects and the people around them. Everything was back to normal. The police were gone. People were back to enjoying their day. Finally, East stood up. Samayah looked up into his caring eyes, waiting for him to say something.

"I hope you get everything in life that your heart desires. You deserve it. And when the day comes for you to go away for school, I'll drive you myself," he said. She smiled but didn't respond. "I'ma go in here and check on your mom," he told her. East put his hand on her shoulder as he walked pass into the apartment.

After he left, Samayah sat there crying some more. What she didn't tell East was that he was part of the reason she was leaving. She had developed such strong feelings for him over the years. As he matured, so did her infatuation. His captivating smile gave her butterflies when he came around. She would stare into his face and get lost in his full lips when he spoke. East wasn't like the other guys their age. He was genuine, reserved but guarded. He had a maturity that exceed his age. Samayah had known him her whole life but he remained an enigma to her. She knew East had love for her, just not the type she wanted him to have. She was deep in love with him. His love was brotherly. That only made it worse to be around him. Samayah knew it was best for her to put some distance between them. She needed to get him out of her system. Going away to college would do just that. She hoped.

CHAPTER ELEVEN

"Ms. James after reviewing the cameras we have identified you as the person responsible for the missing medications. I've reviewed the footage over and over to see if there was any logical explanation for you being in the medicine storage room so many times this month, but there were none. Every time you left the room the inventory count was off. Then footage from two days ago captured you putting bottles of Percocet in your lab coat when you walked out the door. You and I know that is a federal offense. You can get in a lot of trouble for what you did." the doctor was filed with sadness and disappointment. "I've decided not to involve the authorities or the board because I like you Ms. James and I understand you are a single mother raising a son by yourself, but I'm going to have to let you go. Effective immediately."

As Ebony sat on her couch zoned out, replaying the doctor's words, the sound of footsteps snapped her out of the trance.

"Good morning Ma," East greeted, entering the living room and kissing her on the cheek.

Ebony immediately wrapped her arms around him and squeezed him passionately.

"Everything aight?" he asked in confusion.

"Yes. Everything is fine. I can't hug my son." Ebony forged a smile, but it didn't fool him. He could see the sadness in her eyes and could tell something wasn't right. He reached out his arms and pulled her into his tight embrace. He loved her more than life itself. She was his Queen. He promised himself that one day, he would make everything right in her world and give her everything she deserved in life.

East's loving embrace only made Ebony feel worse. She had lost her job a few days ago. Their only source of income and she hadn't told him or anybody yet. She had been caught stealing medications for Lance. Only by the grace of God and the kindness in the doctor's heart, criminal charges were not being pressed. Instead, he terminated her employment. Ebony didn't know what she was going to do. Or how she would get another job with this black cloud hanging over her head.

"Ma, are you sure you're okay?" East pressed noticing her strange behavior. He had never seen a look like that before on her face before. He could see beyond the fake smile.

"Yeah baby, I'm good. You hungry?" she asked, quickly trying to change the subject, managing to subdue her emotions in front of him.

"I'm gonna eat a bowl of cereal."

"Are you sure? I can cook you something."

"Nah, I gotta hurry up and get to the gym."

"Ok, well at least take a shower before you go," she joked.

"I know," he laughed. "I love you," he replied, wrapping his arms around her and kissing her again.

That brought a smile back to Ebony's face. She stared at her son. No matter how bad she felt on the inside, with just one look or one word, he could make her feel whole again. "I love you too."

"You don't have to work today?" he asked.

"No," Ebony lied as a sinking feeling returned to her stomach.

"Well, you need to get out this house today," he said opening the blinds. "Look how nice it is outside."

"Boy, this Miami. It's always nice outside. I don't care about that," she dismissed. "I'ma be right here watching this marathon of First 48," she said. East laughed and shook his head. Ebony watched him walk down the hallway into the bathroom and closed the door.

* * *

"Thanks for lunch," Dos smirked, relaxing his head comfortable on Jasmine's inner thigh. He could still feel her body shivering as they relaxed in the plush hotel bed in the middle of the day. Jasmine was the type of female Dos could get used to. Her sex drive was always in overdrive. She had the looks of a video vixen, the body of an urban Goddess and the feisty attitude of a girl from New York. The combination was breathtaking. He had never been more turned on in his life. He sat up, scanning her body from head to toe.

Jasmine had never had someone to match her sex drive like Dos did. His might have exceeded hers. Every time they had Sex, it was a competiton to see who could please the other more. His oral skills only had left her moaning, groaning and calling for the Lord. She was hot, horny, exhausted but yearned for more pleasure. She sat up and pushed him onto his back. She leaned forward and gave him a passionate kiss, slipping her tongue into his mouth. While their mouths were intertwined together, her hand moved down his body and grabbed his dick. She began to caress it until it was hard again. She swung her leg over him like a ballerina. Straddling him, she began to feed inch after inch of him into her wetness until she had it all inside her. She let out a gasp of satisfaction and began to rock her hips back and forth.

Dos could only lay back and enjoy the ride. His eyes closed. The sound of her phat ass slapping against him filling the room.

"Give me that dick," she shouted. "Give me...all that...fuckin' dick." She was dominant and controlling. Continuing to aggressively bounce up and down on him without stopping.

Dos couldn't take it much longer. He felt his climax approaching like a runaway train. Beads of sweat cover his forehead and began to run down his face. He gripped her ass cheeks, spread them and thrust his hips, trying to match her pump for pump. She accepted the challenge, but he was no match for her on this occasion. She rode him faster and faster.

"Oh shit! I'm bout to cum," he groaned, trying to push her off of him.

Jasmine continued to ride him without stopping.

"Come in this pussy," she cried out as he exploded his thick warm cum inside of her. Jasmine exhaled deeply, collapsing onto his chest. She looked at Dos, he was exhausted, breathing heavily with his eyes closed. She smiled, basking in the moment. "That was good."

"Hell yeah," he smiled.

* * *

"East, you gotta be able to put things out of your mind quickly," Tez explained as they stood in the middle of the ring. He lowered the punching mitts as East stopped punching. He'd noticed East's down demeanor ever since Screw had gotten locked up a week ago. The young man was wearing the stress on his heart and the burden on his shoulders and face. East also couldn't put a finger on what was going on with his mother. Tez would once again have to use boxing to teach a life lesson.

"Look, you might get hit with a punch that shakes you a little bit. You might lose a round here and there. Bad things are going to happen, but you have to get over it quick. Or you'll be a sitting duck." He quickly threw a punch out of nowhere that East avoided and swung back, landing a shot on the body pads Tez wore. "See. It's all about how you react. Now go get your stuff, so I can take you home."

As they drove, East rode shotgun taking in the city. He noticed all older people breaking their necks to speak, while the corner boys grew tense but still showed respect when they rode by. Ricardo got love in the streets but what Tez got felt different. East could sense the fear in others when he came around. It felt deep-rooted.

"Tell me what you see?" Tez asked as he looked over and caught East daydreaming out the window.

"Whatchu mean?"

"Look around you. What do you see?" he repeated pointing out the window.

East stared out at the city as it passed by. He was still a little perplexed by the question. "People," he said, shrugging his shoulders, causing Tez to laugh for one of the few and rare times.

"Nah East, you see opportunity. The world is filled with it. If you can't make money on an earth this big, you deserve to stay broke," Tez explained.

"I ain't tryna be broke," East assured him, and he meant it.

"I already know," Tez smirked. "Check this out," he swiped at his nose, his face growing serious again. "There's a lot of ways to make money. The best and safest way is legally. Get you a job at the Foot Locker or Walmart, something like that," he explained. "But

I know you ain't no dummy. You know a lot more than you say. You see more then you pretend to. I like that about you. And I know I ain't your daddy or nothing. Just do me a favor?" he asked.

"What's that?"

"If you ever decide that you wanna jump out in these streets and get your hands dirty. Come holla at me first," Tez advised. He had a notion about what Dos was up to and how he was getting his product. Tez didn't want East getting involved in none of that. "You got a lot of potential. You can be a world champ someday. I truly believe that. Your fist can take you a long way, but your brain," he said touching his fingers to his head. "It can take you anywhere you want to go," Tez assured him. He pulled up in front of East's apartments and parked. He took the gun off his lap and sat it on the console before reaching into his pocket. He noticed East staring at the gun. "You ever shot one before?" Tez asked suddenly.

"Nah," East replied innocently.

"Ok, tomorrow we gonna change that. Every man should know how to use a gun," Tez declared, his normally raspy voice even more scratchy.

"Why you always ride with it on your lap tho?"

"Things can come at you fast, without warning. You never have to get ready if you stay ready," he schooled, while counting out four $100 bills. "Here," he extended the money to East, who hesitated to take the money. "What's wrong?"

"What's that for?" East didn't like handouts.

"For your pockets."

"I ain't no charity case," East bucked.

Tez chuckled again but not in a funny way. He admired the young boy's defiance. It was just misguided on this occasion. He cut the engine off. "You think I look at you like that?" he asked aggressively, turning his body to face East. His tone rose slightly. "If you think I look at you like that, you don't understand shit I just said. And I know you smarter than that." The words spilled out with the hurt of a father's disappointment. He had too much love for East to look at him as anything less than family.

East nodded his understanding. He could feel the hurt overpowering the anger in Tez's words. "I didn't mean it like that. I just rather earn mines. I never want somebody to feel like I owe them something."

"I understand but..." Tez paused to calm himself. His voice was low when he spoke again. "Sometimes you earn things through respect. I got nothing but love and respect for you, lil' homie, so take it." He once again extended the stack of bills. He figured if he could keep a little money in East's pockets, he could avoid getting into trouble.

"Aight but see now I owe you," East said before taking the money.

"Never count favors. That's hoe shit."

East nodded and gave Tez a pound. "Thanks."

"Aight. I'll see you tomorrow. Bright and early," he reminded East as he got out the car. Tez pulled off.

For some reason, one he could never explain, East paused before unlocking the door to the apartment before walking it. "Ma, I'm home," he called out but received no response. The house was dark and quiet. Unusually quiet. There was always some type of noise in the apartment. Mary J. Blige serenading on low in the background, First 48 Marathon, on the TV, something. His mother even slept with the TV on. But tonight, there was nothing, just absolute silence. "Ma, you here?" he called out again, still no reply "She must've went to work," he said checking his cell phone as he began down the hallway towards her room.

Suddenly, he slipped on something and hit the floor hit hard with a thud, his phone falling from his hand and sliding across the floor. "Ahh," he grunted. "What the..." he griped out loud, realizing his shirt and pants were now wet. That's when he heard the water running and saw the light coming from under the door in the bathroom.

"Ma!" he shouted, jumping up and sprinting to the bathroom door. His feet made splashing sounds in the water with each step. East turned the knob; the door was locked. "Ma! Ma, open the door!" He shouted over and over as he banged on the door repeatedly. Fed up, he lowered his shoulder and rammed it into the door several times until it broke open.

"Aww, no! Ma!" East face disfigured into an ugly cry. He placed both hands on top of his head in shock and disbelief. The sight of his mother's naked body in a tub of overflowing water, with blood streaming from both wrists, almost stopped his heart.

Call 911, he thought to himself, then he shouted it as he pulled her from the tub and onto the floor. "Call 911!" It was like he was telling someone else in the room to do it. But there was no one else. Just him and her, like it had been his whole life. East ran back out into the hallway and located his cell phone. Quickly calling for help as his hand trembled. Re-entering the bathroom, he dropped to his knees beside his mother and held her. "Hold on ma," he pleaded as tears streamed down his face. "They said they're on the way."

Minutes later, East heard the paramedics enter the apartment. "We're in the bathroom," he called out to them.

One paramedic rushed into the bathroom. It looked like a horror flick. Ebony was unresponsive on the floor with a towel covering her body. It looked like her wrist had been ripped out. East moved out the way as paramedic began working on her. He stood in the doorway of the bathroom crying. When he felt a hand on his shoulder. He turned around. It was Tez.

"C'mon, you don't need to see this. Let them do their job. Let's wait outside," He urged East, pulling him away. Tez had seen enough dead bodies for two lifetimes. He knew Ebony was in a bad way.

Soon after, East and Tez stepped outside, the paramedics brought Ebony out the apartment on a stretcher. East followed the paramedics to the ambulance, through a crowd of neighbors and onlookers on their stoops and peering out their windows. They all wore expressions of sadness, anxiousness and fear on their face.

Angela came storming out her house in her robe just as they were putting Ebony in the ambulance. There were tears running down her face and she was screaming frantically, "Nooo!"

Samayah trailed right behind her crying then hugging her mom. She called out to East but he didn't reply or even acknowledge her. For him, it all seemed like a blur. He couldn't even remember getting into the ambulance with his mother or the ride to the hospital. His body was on autopilot.

Tez met them at the hospital. He brought Angela and Samayah along. They sat directly across from him, crying. Samayah rubbed her mother's hand but deep down she wished she was sitting next to East. It broke her heart to see him so hurt. He sat there quietly with blood on his shirt, in a daze with Tez at his side. Soon after, Ricardo and Dos arrived. They were all there to support East. He would need it, not only tonight but moving forward.

One of the doctors came walking into the waiting room. Spotting him, they all rose to their feet with anticipation. Everyone except East. He remained seated with his head down, but he would never forget the words that came out the doctor's mouth. "I'm sorry. She didn't make it."

East felt rage like never before. "What you mean she didn't make it," he barked, catching everyone by surprised as he leaped from his seat. "Go back there and keep working on my mother until she's ok," he shouted, his voice cracking with hurt and pain. He had a huge knot in his stomach. He began to cry hysterically, experiencing all kind of emotions that he had never felt before.

There wasn't a dry eye in the room. Ms. Ang cried for her friend and for East. Samayah couldn't bear to look up as she cried uncontrollably. Ricardo and Dos were bout stunned and had cloudy eyes. Tez had tears in his eyes but showed strength not letting one fall until East walked over to him and look at him with confusion in his teary eyes.

"Why'd she do it, Tez? Why'd she kill herself?" East broke down. "I don't know what to do without her. She just left me by myself," he cried. Tez reached out and hugged him. East buried his head in Tez's chest and they both cried.

After the doctor delivered the devastating news that Ebony had passed, another doctor entered the waiting room minutes later. He offered East the opportunity to see his mother's body. East accepted without hesitation, showing bravery behind his years. With tears in his eyes, he followed the doctor. Entering the room where his mother's body was, East stared at her for a moment them climbed in the bed with her. He rested his head on her. He rubbed her hair. It was soft. He traced his hand across her face, slow and gently like a blind person would to log someone's appearance into their brain. East stayed there for hours, just looking at her, laying with her, not wanting to leave. It was the one thing he could do to make himself feel better. Not leave. Because leaving her, would mean she was really gone, and he wasn't ready to accept that. So, he stayed there, rubbing her hair and kissing her face for hours until finally Tez came in and took him home.

PART III: HEAVY HEART

CHAPTER TWELVE: A YEAR LATER

On the last day of his life, Old Man Al, relaxed on the deck of his yacht, reminiscing and enjoying the beautiful sunset. The sun warmed his face and a gentle breeze carried the smell of salt in from the ocean. He closed his eyes and savored the moment. His deep brown skin glistening with sweat. His handsome face covered with unshaved grey stubbles. A true vet in the Miami drug game, if there ever was one. Al was the man that had made it snow in paradise for years. The plug. The gatekeeper, with the power to decide who was able to come through those gates. There was a time when if Al gave you his blessing, you were on, in a major way. He could flood the streets, or just as easily turn off the faucets and starve them because his dope supply was feeding over 25 cities in Florida and a couple surrounding states. He had single-handedly given birthed to the next generation of Miami hustlers, making millions and millionaires in the process. He also kept the peace in the streets. That was all before he derailed his own empire with gambling and cocaine addiction. Al lost his discipline and it cost him his connect. Only because of years of doing good business had his connect decided to spare his life. Instead of being dealt a death sentence, Al was cut off and dried out completely. Exiled from the game he had once played so well. That didn't curve his addictions. Eventually he swindled away most of the possessions he'd earned in the drug game. All except for his prized fifty-foot yacht that now doubled as his home. Al looked around and a smirked creased his lips as he summoned memories of his glory days in the game. Thoughts of the lucrative business deals he'd closed right on the deck of his yacht. The parties with beautiful women as they sailed around the waters of Miami at night. The money, the drugs, the sex, the lifestyle. He once had it all and enjoyed it to the fullest; a little too much.

Al removed the Panama-style straw hat from his head and wiped the sweat from his brow. He placed the hat on the table, next to a pile of cocaine. He lowered his face into it and sniffed the coke off the table, using his nose like a vacuum cleaner. Over his years in the game, Al had developed an insatiable appetite for cocaine. No longer able to balance or control his habit, it drove his impulsive decisions and fed into his constant state of paranoia. He felt like someone was out to get him. Al overindulged in everything that was his downfall. When it came to the streets, gambling or drugs, too much was never enough. He'd always been that way. It made him a legend. It earned him a nickname amongst childhood friends that would stick for the rest of his life. Since he was the first one to jump off the porch. The first one getting money in his circle. The first to meet a plug and see a brick. The first one buying foreign cars and diamonds. It made him seem older then he was, even to the guys his own age, so they named him Old Man Al. But the fast life was unforgiving. When it finally caught up, it destroyed him and everything around him. Now he was just a washed-up, paranoid nigga on a boat, holding on to what was left of his glory days. And suffering from PTSD from the dope game.

"Aaah," he growled from the rush of the coke entering his nostrils, leaning back in his chair with the look of a rabid dog in his eyes. Al used his finger to wipe residue from the table, then licked his fingertip like it was dipped in barbeque sauce. He washed it down with a swig of cognac then continued enjoying the view.

This place could really give a man a false sense of security, he thought to himself about Miami. The sunny weather, moderate temperatures and clear blue waters *gave most people the feeling that they were safer than they really were. It was just an illusion, a beautiful distraction from the dangers that were always close by. Al knew that better than most. He had experienced both triumph and tragedy here. The highest highs and the lowest lows. He enjoyed the water, spending most of his time on it. Fishing off his yacht in the middle of Biscayne Bay most days. It was what he had been reduced to doing. Still, it was his tranquil place but just like the rest of Miami, there were always a million things brewing right under the serene surface. There was a war coming. A power struggle in the streets that he had avoided during his reign. Al did business with everyone equally back then. It kept the peace. Everybody ate, so everyone was happy. That wasn't the case anymore. Miami was in turmoil. The streets were in chaos. Rival crews vying for the crown he left behind. His removal from the top had caused a power vacuum. And it would surely get bloodier before it got better.*

His jaw tightened as he stared at Downtown Miami's skyline. I used to own this fucking city. The thought angered him causing an aching to swell in his chest, forcing him to sniff away tears. He sighed deeply then gulped down the rest of his cognac. Al stared into the empty glass, seeming lost in his thoughts, allowing the hurt he felt to build inside. Suddenly he screamed, letting out all his frustration then tossed the glass across the boat, shattering it on impact. The mixture of failure and cocaine in his system fueling his outburst. He could no longer numb the pain. There wasn't a drug powerful enough to dull the shame he felt on the inside. It ate at him daily. This evening it made him not want to go on living. His vices and addictions had reduced him to a shell of himself. All he did was fish, snort coke, drink and sleep. He was a poor excuse for a man. So, he decided the world would be better off without him in it.

He snatched the gun off the table, ready to get it over with but it was false courage because he immediately put it back down. Unable to come to terms with his fate. Al bit down on his fist as tears began to rain from down his cheek. "I don't think I can do this," he doubled over in agony, crying aloud. Taking a life was one thing, he had done that before but taking his own, How? How was he supposed to do this? How had he fallen this far? He looked to the sky and asked God, Why? And swore he felt God look away from him in shame. Al sobbed harder, until he was drained of every tear he had. His body and mind were exhausted. He straightened his posture in the chair. Bring himself back upright then reluctantly, reaching for the gun again. When he felt the rubber grip in his hand, he became nauseous, vomit tickling the back of his throat. He had to fight to keep it down, ignoring the feeling. He lifted the gun off the table. His hand shaking the whole time. He pressed it to the side of his head, unable to stop the sobs that were spilling out of him. This was it; the Grand Finale. There was a hesitation in his trigger finger that had never been there before; trepidation really. A moment of cold feet causing a silence to fill in the air. Al lowered the gun from his head and stuck it in his mouth. There was a still in the evening that was immediately followed by a gunshot. The single blast echoing loudly through the air, disturbing the calm, causing a flock of seagulls nearby to fly away. Their squawking overhead muting out the thud of the gun falling from Al's dead hand as his head crushed face down on the table. His lifeless eyes still open, brains and blood leaking everywhere.

The beautiful long-stemmed rose in Lauryn's trembling hand, paled in comparison to the flawless diamond on the same hand she clutched it in. Her heart was heavy and aching as she stood in front of the beautifully sculpted statue of a weeping angel, hugging her father's headstone, replaying his death in her mind. Lauryn had been to her father's gravesite hundreds of times in the past five years. She came dressed in black like always. The same way she had on the day of his funeral. Every time she made him the same promise. Every time it felt like it was the first time she had been to visit. It was like picking the scab off a wound. The initial pain would return as soon as she pulled up in front of the cemetery gates. After losing her father, there was something inside of her that would never heal. The memory of his death would start playing in her mind before she could even get out the car. It had been the worst day of her life and the most pain she had ever felt. Even now, five years later, it was still a crippling feeling. She felt sick just being there. She placed her hand over her midsection as she felt it lurch. Her chest threatening to cave in as she fought back tears, trying to find the words to say, even though they were always the same.

"I miss you so much, daddy," a mournful cry escaped her lips, grief consuming her. She keeled over, falling to her knees, hugging the headstone tightly before tracing her fingers over it.

East stood a few feet away, silent, dressed in all black as well. His young features were stoic, his handsome face remaining in a hard expression. His hand close to the gun on his waist. He was there to do his job. Guarding was the boss' wife. Ricardo had entrusted him to keep his most prized possession safe. He was close enough to protect her if needed, but not close enough to invade her privacy. His natural instinct was to offer her comfort. It bothered him to see her broken, and in such pain, but he knew better. He knew to keep his distance. Still, East found himself staring at her in admiration. Even in such sadness, her beauty was rare. It delighted the eyes. Her glow was radiant. It was like the sun lived in the lining of her skin. Her full lips and doe like eyes had put men twice his age in a trance. She could have any nigga in the city if she wanted. She had always appeared regal to East. Putting on a brave face for the world to see. But in that moment, her willingness to be vulnerable in front of him allowed him to see how delicate she really was. He turned his face away, ashamed that he was witnessing such a private, emotional moment. He thought it better if he waited for her by the car. She didn't even notice him step away.

"Ain't you supposed to be her shadow?" the driver asked East. "You a lil' too far away if you ask me."

"Ain't nobody asked you," East countered.

"Ricardo'll kill your lil' ass if anything happens to her," the driver chuckled then blew out a cloud of cigarette smoke. Everybody knew how serious Ricardo was about Lauryn. She didn't go anywhere without protection.

"She deserves to grieve in private," East responded.

"I'm just saying—"

"You talkin' a little too much. Thought they paid you to drive?" East's cold stare put an end to their conversation. The driver tossed his cigarette to the ground, circled the truck and got behind the wheel. Despite his young age, East was well respect within the organization. He was like Tez's son and a second son to Ricardo. Both men held him in deep regards. East leaned against the hood of the SUV and waited patiently for Lauryn to finish.

There was a time when Lauryn felt like she had the world on a string. Her whole life was in front of her then. She had been so confident, so full of cheer. That seemed so long ago. She hadn't even fully entered womanhood when her father died. She hadn't known the rules. Now at 26 years old, she was no longer a bright-eyed young girl. She was well versed in the workings of the underworld. Her youthful innocence had been violently snatched away, leaving behind a woman hardened by grief and anger, nothing but collateral damage of the drug game. She rested her head against the headstone and whispered to her father, words only meant for his ears.

Until then, the sky had been perfect, but it was quickly changing. Miami's weather was funny like that. The beautiful blue shade was turning into a hard grey. Large pillows of cloud beginning to form, blocking out the sun. A gust of wind blew, stirring the trees then Lauryn heard a pitter patter as the first pearls of rain dropped onto the leaves. The rainfall suddenly became more intense, mixing with the trail of tears streaming down her face. She laid the rose on top of the headstone then walked towards her waiting ride. East met her more than halfway, providing her shelter from the rain underneath an umbrella. The drops were drumming against the ground nonstop as they made it to her car. East reached out, opening the door for her and helping her in. Once she was safely inside, he slammed the door shut behind her, closed the umbrella and got into the front passenger seat of the black Lincoln Navigator.

Lauryn sat in the back composing herself, wiping away the remaining tears while looking at her reflection in a compact mirror. Her beautiful face hid the hurt well behind designer labels and foreign cars. She forged a smile as her eyes met East's and he told the driver to start the engine. Suddenly, the sun came out again, casting slanted beams of light across the cemetery. Steam rose slowly from the grass. It rose up eerily and drifted mist-like towards the golden sun. The image was so vivid that it stayed with

Lauryn for the rest of the day. She took it as a sign that things would get better. "After the rain, the sun will shine again," she mumbled to herself.

"Huh?" East asked looking over his shoulder at here.

"Nothing," she quickly dismissed. "We can go now," she instructed. After visiting her father's grave there was only one thing in the world that could brighten her spirits. A little retail Therapy.

* * *

For East, pulling up to Ricardo's new home felt like he was in another world. Palm Island was only a fifteen-minute drive from where he grew up in Liberty City. Despite the short distance, the places couldn't have been further from apart. The exclusive waterfront neighborhood was home to the stars. There was lush landscaping throughout the entire island and beautiful water features that connect the properties to its natural environment fronting Biscayne Bay. Ricardo had recently purchased a 6,800 square foot, island style home with a pool and boat dock attached at the rear.

Arriving through the gate, the circular courtyard had stone pavers, grouted with lawn and a fountain in the middle, creating a striking scenery. A few foreign vehicles adorned the driveway, along with a fleet of tinted out SUVs. Two large palm trees stood like pillars near the front of the mansion, adding to the appeal of the property. Ricardo, Tez and Dos, stood out front engaged in a conversation. To East it felt like a scene out of a movie. He got out the truck and opened the back door for Lauryn.

"Thank you," she said in a sweet tone as he helped her out the seat. She smiled but her eyes didn't. There was so much pain laying behind her exterior, right there in the windows to her soul.

"You alright?" East inquired, his nature wouldn't let him ignore what he saw.

"I'll be fine, East. Thanks for asking," she replied in a somber tone. It was rare that any of her husband's workers said a word to her. Most were afraid to even make eye contact with the boss' beautiful wife. Not East. He was different, he always said, "Good morning" when she passed or "Goodnight" when he left. He always acknowledged her presence. Lauryn appreciated his humbleness and enjoyed his presence when he accompanied her places. Ricardo's other workers were like robots in suits. East had a youthful innocence that hadn't been hardened by the world yet. She admired it but at the same time was a bit envious, recalling when she saw the world like he did. Lauryn spotted Ricardo's observant eyes on her. She cut her eyes wickedly at him and sauntered in the house. East retrieved the bags from her shopping spree and followed her into the house.

"Wifey look pissed. What you did now?" Tez questioned.

Ricardo shrugged, barely acknowledged her behavior and refusing to entertain the conversation. He knew Lauryn was spoiled and because of that she wasn't going anywhere. Not in a million years. She always returned from visiting her father's gravesite with a cloud of sadness surrounding her. It was nothing an expensive gift couldn't cheer up. Ricardo and Tez continued to talk and walk, leaving Dos behind.

"Look at you, nigga," Dos laughed as East appeared from the front door. "You look like the secret service," he quipped, brushing imaginary lent from East's suit. "When you gonna stop with all Alfred shit," referring to the character famous for being Batman's butler. "And come get some real money with ya boy?" Dos asked. He was draped up and dripped out. Gucci down with a big Cuban link chain hanging from his neck and diamonds in his ear. He had stepped up to doing pickups for his father but was still conducting his side business under Ricardo's nose.

"I ain't missing nothing," East proclaimed. He moved at his own pace. He wasn't interested in keeping up with the Joneses or in this case Dos Wheeler.

"You really need to step your car game up G," Dos teased, walking over to his brand new white Mercedes S-Coupe, a birthday gift from his father. While Dos preferred luxury and the status that came with driving foreigns, East drove an old school.

"This a classic. American muscle. Whenever you ready to put your car to the test, let me know," he challenged as he stood next to his 1966 Chevy Impala. He removed his suit and tie, tossing it in the backseat and began changing clothes.

"You coming to my party tonight, right? It's gonna be a lot of bitches in there," Dos offered.

"Nah bro. You know the club ain't my thing. Plus, I got something to do."

"Nigga, what could possibly be more important than my birthday party?"

"I made a promise to someone I gotta keep. Have a good time. Happy Birthday my nigga!" East said slamming his door, chucking a deuce and pulling off.

Ricardo and Tez watched the two young men drive away like proud fathers.

"I got word on the nigga Lance," Ricardo said. Both men had become aware of Lance's dealings with Ebony. Ricardo reached out through some back channel and found out he was the reason she lost her job, which led to her committing suicide. They both wanted to make it right for East.

"I'll take care of it, ASAP," Tez said without hesitation.

"East been doing a good job keeping Lauryn safe, but I think it's time for him to step up," Ricardo stated, rubbing his hand over his beard. He like everyone else saw the potential in East and thought it was time for him to get his hands dirty.

"I don't think he ready yet," Tez replied. "I'll take care of it." Tez repeated.

"Fuck you mean, he not ready?" Ricardo shot back. "That was his mother. Wouldn't you wanna be the one who did it, if it was your mother?" he asked but didn't give Tez a chance to respond. "He more ready then any of these lil' niggas on the team. If he ain't, he better get ready."

"I don't think that's a good idea," Tez shrugged.

"Why not?"

"I don't see you sending Dos out there on no murder missions," Tez was making it clear how he viewed East. It had just become clear Ricardo didn't quite see it the same way.

Ricardo eyed him with suspicion. "I don't have any doubts about Dos. He's my son," his voice raising with excitement. "You act like you're East's daddy or something," he said. Tez had become a little too attached to East. He was becoming too overprotective. "You killed his daddy, remember? You ain't his daddy," Ricardo reminded him.

"You got selective memory I see. Cause I did that for you," Tez gritted his teeth. "Because you couldn't, remember? The connect would have killed you too. They told you to do it. You couldn't. So, I did."

"What are you saying?" Ricardo shot back angrily as he got in Tez's face. "If you got an issue, you need to see a therapist. Otherwise, get over that shit. Cause I ain't a therapist and I ain't running a daycare. I'm in the drug business, nigga. I got thorough niggas on my team. I bred em that way. I've bred them to be loyal and to put in work. And I'm gonna put them to good use, all of them. Shit, these houses and cars ain't gonna pay for themselves, Tez."

"I hear a lot of I's and My's when you talk lately. Don't forget who helped you build all this bro," Tez replied. When shit hit the fan, it was always him on the front line not Ricardo. Tez knew in his heart East was ready. He was more ready than even Ricardo knew. He just wanted to protect him from the life and keep him away from the game as long as he could. Tez had been in the streets long enough to know that it changed people. Some in worse ways than others. He witnessed it first-hand. He had killed plenty men, including East's father. Many on the word of Ricardo and their ghost haunted him, especially Derek Eastwood's. He had gotten use to not sleeping peacefully at night. He was a hustler, but he was also a killer, and killers killed. It was what he had signed up for once he took his first life. Maybe he had gotten too attached to East but so what, he loved him. Tez had seen and done so much, he didn't wish his life on anyone, certainly not East.

"What the fuck that mean?" Ricardo barked.

"Forget it," Tez answered.

"Nah, say what's on ya mind. You feeling a way?" Ricardo could see the averse in Tez's eyes. He didn't like the fact that his authority was being questioned.

"I just don't think East is ready, that's all," Tez repeated.

"He ready cause I said he ready," Ricardo asserted with a finality that ended the conversation.

CHAPTER THIRTEEN

East removed the last box from the backseat of the car and closed the door. The college campus was 500 miles away from Liberty City, but it could have easily been five thousand miles away as far as East was concerned. He looked around as he carried the large box down a walkway, there were students dressed in Green and Orange walking around everywhere. He caught the eyes of some female students as he passed. East entered Polkinghorne Village East and headed up the stairs.

"What you got in here, your whole life?" he asked as he entered Samayah's room.

"Basically," she shrugged as she stole in the middle of the floor, scanning the room. "Put it over there," she directed.

Samayah was now a freshman at FAMU in Tallahassee. She had grown into a beautiful young woman. She wasn't petite at all. She was thick, well fed with shapely hips, thick thighs and a big round ass. Her stomach wasn't flat, it still had a little pudge, leftover baby fat from being a chubby little girl but it was tight. She was rocking a crop top and cut up jeans and Jordans. Her honey brown skin was now clear of the blemishes that had once plagued her as a teen. Her long, black hair looked like weave, but it wasn't. Her eyebrows were perfectly arched and her nails freshly manicured.

"Damn," East huffed as he put the box down.

Samayah smiled innocently as she bit on her nail. She had put him to work and East had worked up a sweat. She eyed the boxes and quickly opened one, reaching in and tossing him a washcloth. "Here."

"Thank you," he replied catching it mid-air and wiping his brow. He smiled.

Samayah stared lustfully, getting lost for a moment in his pearly whites. She caught herself and refocused. "No, thank you for keeping your word. It means a lot."

"I wanted to. This meant a lot to me too."

"Really, why?"

"Cuz I'm proud of you," he admitted. "You're the first person I know that's going to college. That shit don't happen where we're from. My mom went to Everest but—." His words trailed off and he went quiet. He looked down at his feet then back up at her. "I'm proud of you, that's all."

Samayah knew his mother's death was a sore spot. A whole year had passed, and East hadn't been back to the gravesite since the funeral. He hardly mentioned Ebony's name. He never talked about her death or anything related to her. It was like he had wiped his mother from his memories. He resented her for what she did. In his mind, she was selfish for killing herself and leaving him alone in the world, to deal with the pain and unanswered questions.

Samayah walked over and sat down next to him. She put her hand on top of his. "You should go see her, East," she suggested softly.

"That's not open for discussion," he quickly dismissed the subject, stood up and walked across the room.

"Why not?" Samayah protested, rising to her feet. "That's your mother. Your mother, East. I, of all people know how much she meant to you and how much you meant to her."

"I just said I'm not talking about that with you,"

he barked.

"We'll if not with me then talk to somebody," she pleaded. "Are you really that messed up, that you can't allow someone to be nice to you? And try to help you?" she asked. "You can't continue to walk around with all that hurt bottled up inside. It'll kill you. It's changing you already. You're different than you used to be—"

"Since when you became such an expert on me?" he challenged.

"Oh, you wouldn't believe how much of an expert I am on you, Eastwood James." Her voice rose to match his as she stood up, marched across the room and pointed her finger at him. "I know you have the smallest mole on the outside of your right hand. I know your ears go up and down when you smile," she paused, closed her eyes to see it in her mind, "And I think it's the cutest thing ever," she smiled. "I know you bite the inside of your jaw when you're in deep thought. I know you prefer cheesecake on your birthday because you hate frosting. And you love root bear. And your favorite basketball player is D. Rose even though he's always hurt, you won't give up on him because your loyal. So, don't tell me I'm not an expert on you because I am. And I have been. Because I've been in love with you ever since we were kids," Samayah confessed then kissed him.

East pulled back, reached out and grabbed her hands, then he looked into her teary eyes and said sincerely, "I love you too, Samayah, but—"

"Not like that, right?" she finished his sentence and snatched her hands away from him. She walked over to the bed and sat down as tears began to fall down her face.

"You're my best friend's sister."

"East I know, please, don't remind me," she said upsettingly as she used her hands to wipe the tears.

"Samayah, listen to me. You're going places that I'm not. This college shit is your key to a new life. You should find somebody here, at school. You shouldn't even like niggas like me. There are better guys for you. A future lawyer or a doctor, somebody like that. Anybody but me."

"I don't care about none of that, East. I love you," she expressed as the tears started to fall again. Nothing he could say would change how she felt. Her heart wanted what it wanted.

"You gotta get that out your head," he explained calmly.

"Why do you think I wanted to go away for school? It's the only way I can get you out my head.

Because seeing you every day and being around you, only makes things worse for me." East reached and tried to give her a hug, but she pushed him away. "Just leave," she demanded.

"Samayah."

"Just leave, East."

He sighed and rubbed his hand over his head. He bit the inside of his jaw as he stood there staring at her. Finally, he spoke, "Call me if you need anything—"

"I won't," she said with attitude.

East walked over to the door and let himself out.

After he left, Samayah walked over to a chair beside the window. She sat there crying, watching from her window as East got in his car and pulled off. In the quietness of her new residence, Samayah sat there hurting and crying rivers of tears.

* * *

Ain't this what they been waiting for?

Meek Mill's voice sent the crowd inside of Club Liv into a frenzy as the intro of *Dreams and Nightmares* came blaring through the club speakers. Dos stood in VIP with a bottle of champagne in his hand, Jasmine at his side and his crew surrounding them. Dos' was dripped out. Gucci down with a big Cuban link chain hanging from his neck, a Patek on his wrist and diamonds in his ear. He sipped from the bottle then sang along.

I used to pray for times like this, to rhyme like this
So I had to grind like that, to shine like this

Rio sat on the back of the couch in VIP with a bottle in their hand. He joined in.

Seen my dreams unfold, nightmares come true
It was time to marry the game and I said, yeah I do

"Yeah nigga!" Dos shouted as he walked over to Rio and put his arm around him "You babysittin'?"

Rio looked down at the half empty champagne bottle in his hand and laughed before sipping it. Club Liv was packed. Ricardo had rented out the club for Dos' 21st Birthday. The scene was straight out of a rap video. There were half-naked bottle girls in skimpy bathing suits, all around the VIP, carrying buckets of bottles as sparklers flew.

"Happy Birthday, cuz," Rio smiled.

"You see that shit?" Dos asked, tapping his cousin on the low. "That bitch got that fattest ass in here," he nodded towards a female dancing in their section. The curvy woman glanced over her shoulder at him and smiled.

"You better chill nigga before Jaz fuck you up in here," Rio reminded him. "She's looking this way right now," he teased jokingly.

Dos laughed as he looked over at Jasmine. She was heated, wearing her emotions on her sleeve as usual. He could hear her voice in his head cursing him out, *sneaky ass.* "She'll be alright," he dismissed.

"If you ain't talkin' bout my niggas then what you talkin' bout," Rio chanted joyfully raising his bottle in the sky.

Rio was Dos' cousin. He was what the streets referred to as a smart dumb nigga, highly intelligent but prone to making bad decisions. But Dos loved him.

"Yo, I almost forgot, the nigga Kev said he needed to holla at you fam," he said.

"Right now?" Dos asked.

"He said it's important."

"Where he at?" Dos asked. When Rio pointed to Kev across the VIP, Dos motioned for him to take a walk with him. When they were clear of the noise, Dos inquired about the urgency of this meeting. "What's going on Kev?"

"My brother Blue is coming home soon," Kev sounded nervous.

"And?" Dos asked.

"And he's gonna want to get money like he used to, before he went away." Kev confessed.

"Things ain't like they used to be," Dos stated firmly.

"I know that, but he might not see it like that."

"That's on you, Kev," Dos shrugged. "If you don't want to fuck up the gravy train we got going, you gotta handle that." Dos shifted in his stance. "Get him straight when he touches down. A crib, a whip, some bread. Tell me him welcome home, enjoy his freedom a lil' bit. It's a new day out here on these streets," Dos explained with a chuckle.

"I respect all that but Blue's a hustler and a gangster by nature. I can't make him sit on his hands. He can't stay still too long." Kev informed him.

"Can't stay still? Nigga just did 5 years sitting still." Dos joked. "C'mon playboy. He gotta understand, you're running things now. No more of that lil' brother shit. You had this shit in motion way before he was coming home. It's hard to plug a nigga in from behind the wall. Trust me, it's gonna be all good," he assured. "Another thing, from now on, you gonna be dealing directly with my cousin, Rio."

"Why the sudden change?" Kev asked.

"I got my reasons," Dos said, unwilling to explain further. "Trust me, he's gonna take care of you, my nigga. But it's my birthday," Dos said with excitement sipping his bottle. "I ain't really worried about none of that right now. You feel me?"

"Yeah, I feel you. Happy Birthday my G," Kev said. The two friends embraced before heading back into the VIP area.

Upon re-entering Dos made his way across the room and snuck up behind Jasmine who was standing talking to some of her friends. He put his arms around her waist and rested his hands on her pregnant belly. "Why you standing over here looking all mad," he said softly into her ear while kissing on her neck.

"Cuz you think you're slick," she huffed.

"What you talkin bout ma?" he charmed.

"Dos, your sneaky ass knows exactly what I'm talkin' bout"

"Stop acting crazy and dance with me," he said rocking her back and forth to the music. He kissed her neck. They danced song after song, celebrating another year of life for Dos and the life growing in her stomach. The fact that Dos had the closest people to him around him made it even more special.

Jasmine kissed Dos passionately as white and gold balloons fell from the ceiling. "Happy Birthday baby. I love you," she said.

"I love you more," he replied.

"How much longer you trying to be here?" she asked feeling the bulge in his pants rubbing against her.

"Not much longer," he said, squeezing her butt pulling her close to him kissing her again.

* * *

Tez's anger still had the best of him. Ricardo's ego was getting out of hand. In his heart, Tez felt things would get worse before they got better. He backed into a parking spot, turned off his car and sat back, taking in the scene. He had come a long way from chasing nickels and dimes, day and night, grinding hard, sleeping in trap houses. His only goal back then was to get money. He came from the trances, getting it out the mud, while Ricardo was off chasing Olympic medals. Now Ricardo was behaving like he was his boss. Tez didn't need a boss. He just didn't like the spotlight or mind playing second fiddle. But Ricardo had let that go to his head. Tez leaned back against the headrest and rubbed his eyes with the palms of his hands. The obvious was the obvious for a reason. Maybe it was time to get out the game. It had been a good run. Ricardo was his closest friend in the world. He would hate for something to change that. All the while, Tez was studying the scene and reading faces.

Lance pulled his BMW up in front of the Ray's pool hall & wing hut. Expensive cars were parked all around the popular hangout. He was starving and was dying to get some of Ray's famous hot wings. He exited the car and vanished inside.

As he entered the spot, Lance was greeted by the cute, black female behind the counter. "Hey, Lance," she flirted.

"What's up ma," he replied. "I called in an order for pick up. 10 hot wings. All flats and an orange soda," he said.

"I got you right here, honey," the woman said turning and grabbing a Styrofoam contained and putting it in a plastic bag. "Ranch or Blue Cheese?"

"Ranch. Let me get an extra one too," he said then paid his tab. Lance walked out the front door of the spot and got in his car. His stomach was growling. He couldn't wait for the ride home he needed a few wings now. He removed the container from the bag and opened it. Focusing on Ray's famous wings, Lance never seen Tez creep up on his car.

BOOM! BOOM! BOOM!

The sound of gunshots sent everyone scattering. The bright flashes lighting up the inside of the car. The powerful blast entered Lance's head just behind his left ear. The bullets burst through his head before exiting through his face. The force of the shot blew the back of his head off along with a portion of his brain. The blood splattered all over the dashboard. His body slumped over, blood spilling from the back of his head. For Tez, it was personal. That was for East. He calmly tucked the gun and walked back to his car. Easily blending in with the traffic racing out the parking lot.

CHAPTER
FOURTEEN

It was after midnight when Ricardo decided to summon East to meet with him. After entering the office of his boxing gym, Ricardo sat behind a desk preparing to make the call. The walls of the office were covered with old fight posters, Sonny Liston versus Cassius Clay, Duran versus Leonard, to name a few. Ricardo picked up his cell phone and dialed. He had no contacts stored, just a knack for remembering numbers. He would have called from the office phone, except it was tapped. So was the other line in the gym. He knew it but kept them that way to mislead cops and any other unwanted listeners.

Across town, inside his bedroom, East lay awake in the bed with a cloud of weed smoke dancing above him. The only light in the room came from the TV. A rerun episode of Martin was playing but he wasn't paying it any mind. Samayah was on his brain.

East wasn't blind. He noticed her. Samayah was beautiful. Not only was she very attractive but she had the brains to compliment her looks. How could he not have noticed but she was off limits, so he suppressed those feelings. She was his best friend's sister. They had grown up either next door to each other or under the same roof for most of their lives. Ms. Ang had let East move in after his mother died. He had been to all Samayah's family functions, attended all her graduations since elementary school. He had driven her to college on her first day. Her own mother called him, "Nephew." *He couldn't be with her*, he told himself.

Suddenly, his phone rang on the nightstand, grabbing his attention. He ashed the weed. "What's up?" he said answering on the third ring.

"Eastwood." Ricardo was still the only person that had ever called East by his whole name, so instantly he knew who the voice on the phone belonged to. "I need to see you."

"Can it wait? It's like 2 in the morning," East

explained, uninterested in getting out of his bed. It had already been a long day, having to drive Samayah to college in Tallahassee.

"Nah, it can't. I need to see you right now," Ricardo's tone was serious and firm. "It's important. My guys are waiting outside for you," he declared.

East sat up in the bed. It was almost two in the morning. *What was so important that Ricardo had sent his men to his apartment,* he thought to himself. Something didn't feel right. He got out the bed and went into the living room with his gun in his hand. East walked over to the window and looked outside. He spotted Ricardo's men exactly where he said they would be. In front of his apartment, standing in front of a black SUV.

"You still there?" Ricardo broke the long pause.

"Yeah, I'm here," East answered in a low voice. "You wanna give me a heads up on what's this about?"

"You'll find out when you get here," Ricardo replied with finality then the line went dead.

East let the phone linger by his ear for a moment before he lowered it. He wasn't sure what the fuck was happening. All he knew was something wasn't right. He was caught off guard by the phone call and the tone of the conversation. Ricardo had always preferred to avoid the phone altogether. He usually handed down orders two men deep, to ensure that nothing could be traced back to him. He was old school but the fact that he had made the call himself, had East's mind racing. He got dressed in a hurry and went outside where Ricardo's stone-faced goons awaited him. An awkward silence came over them as he approached. Before he could get closer, they halted his progress by surrounding him. One of the henchmen stepped forward and patted him down, removing the gun from underneath his hoodie.

"I'm gonna hold on to this," he said tucking East's gun into his own waist.

"What's going on?" East asked but the henchmen didn't respond before making him get in the waiting truck. East remained calm as he rode in the backseat next to one of the goons. He didn't say a word. Peering out the back window, he could see another truck, filled with more of Ricardo's men following them as well. He had no idea what was going on but if they were trying to scare him, it wasn't working. He didn't scare easily.

The driver rolled to a stop in an alley behind the gym. East got out and so did everyone in the cars that had pulled in behind them. When he turned and saw them all, an electric bolt of energy surged through his body. Hostile looks on the faces of each men fueled the tension in the air. He had come up with a few of them in Ricardo's gym, now they were all dressed in black, the color of death. East stared in each of their eyes, looking for the one who would be bold enough to step up. He was ready for whatever, trying to guess how it would happen but to his surprise, no one made a move on him. He couldn't understand why they were standing there passively watching but he noticed there was one face conspicuous in its absence.

"Yo, where's Tez?" East asked to no one in particular.

"Don't worry about that," one of the henchmen replied before nudging him forward, towards the back entrance.

The gym was dimly lit and eerily silent when East entered. It felt like the temperature had suddenly dipped, a cold chill sweeping over him. At first, there was only the sound of his own footsteps then floating in from the back of the gym, the faint murmur of voices. In the distance, East spotted more of Ricardo's men. They appeared to be enjoying a laugh. As he came into the light, East spotted Tez, on a stool in the middle of the gym, hunched over, staring at his shoes like an athlete removed from a game that was hopelessly lost. His face was bloodied and battered. His jaw looked grotesque, swelling a great deal from the beating he had suffered. His lips were moving but whatever he was saying East couldn't understand it.

Next to Tez, Ricardo leaned against the ring's apron with both hands in the pockets of the Adidas tracksuit he wore. His sleeves were rolled up, his diamond faced, gold Rolex on full display. Although his attire was understated, his piercing eyes exuded power and his strong presence could be felt by all in the gym. Now almost 40, Ricardo sported a freshly shaved bald head and a thick, full beard. He had gained a small potbelly since his fighting days. In a weird way it enhanced his boss like appearance. He was eating in the streets. A *money gut*, he called it.

East could never forget the first time he walked into the gym. He was just a kid, *thirteen or maybe fourteen*, he thought to himself. He had a similar feeling that day as he did right now.

Back then the community saw Ricardo as a positive influence on the neighborhood kids. Little did any of them know, the gym was his own personal breeding ground. He had spawned the next generation of cocaine cowboys. His own personal army of killers and dealers, who had pledged their undying loyalty to him.

But that was then, and this was now. Ricardo, flanked closely by Dos, slowly began to circle Tez on the stool. He took his time, wanting to choose his words carefully. Everyone held their breath waiting for him to speak. When he finally did, his husky voice was cold and calculated.

"I knew dis' nigga here since the sandbox. That's longer than most of you been alive. But I got a feeling y'all gonna outlive my man, Tez," Ricardo said while never taking his eyes off of East. "My momma had a saying, *scratch a lie, find a thief.* Meaning if a nigga'll lie to you, he'll steal from you and if he'd steal from you, he'd kill you," he explained, circling Tez with his hands still in his pocket.

Tez never looked up. Even when Ricardo placed a hand on his shoulder and smiled. A gesture of twisted reassurance that he was going to be dead very soon. Like a sledgehammer to the chest, it hit East what was happening. Tez had somehow crossed Ricardo and now he was going to kill him and maybe anybody close to him. East cursed under his breath, knowing that meant his fate was probably sealed too. Tez was not only his mentor but he had become like a father figure to him. He held him in higher regards then he did Ricardo himself.

Ricardo walked over and stood directly in front

of him. The two of them, toe to toe and eye to eye. "You know what I hate worse than a liar?" he asked rhetorically. "A disloyal ass thief!" Ricardo's voice echoed through the gym.

There was complete silence. Ricardo was so close that East could hear him breathing. *A thief?* East thought to himself.

"Yeah, a thief. A fuckin' thief," Ricardo said like he had read East's thoughts.

Hell no, East thought to himself. In all the years he had been around him, he had never witnessed any type of disloyalty from Tez. He strongly doubted what was being said about his mentor. Although he had to admit, Tez had to be angered by the nepotism that was soon to make Dos second-in-command within the organization over him. After all, Tez had helped build Ricardo into a powerful man on the streets of Miami, when Dos was still a little boy. During war times, the threat of letting Tez off the leash became a major part of their organization's mystique. And intimidation sometimes, was a better weapon than a gun. Even with all that, East could never see Tez pulling a move like that. *Kill Ricardo and takeover, maybe...but steal...Nah,* he thought to himself.

"This has been going on for some time now,"

Ricardo explained. "My product has been coming up missing, a little here and a little there. You wouldn't know anything about that, would you?" If Ricardo asked a question, he most likely already knew the answer.

East had always been good at tests and his gut feeling was telling him something bigger was in play. "Nah," he answered.

"You sure about that?" Ricardo pressed, clearly trying to read him.

"Very sure," East answered strongly. There was no change in his demeanor or dent in his conviction. He had already accepted there was a chance he wouldn't make out of there alive. He had nothing to lose, so he spoke his mind. "I don't think Tez would do—"

Ricardo cut him off with a look. He could be a very intimidating person but as he searched East's eyes, he found no fear or deception, only the truth. "You always been a solid lil' nigga, Eastwood," he said, putting his hand on East's shoulder. Ricardo saw him as likeable and shrewd for his age with tons of heart. He was as tough as Dos but with none of the recklessness.

"I wanna see what you really made of," Ricardo declared, removing a Glock .40 from his waist. "Kill

Tez," he instructed. Ordering murder effortlessly like it was a number 3 on a fast food menu. His eyes piercing through East as he handed him the gun.

Ricardo's words lingered in the air for a moment. He knew how close East was to Tez. He wanted to break that bond. He was the boss, the only voice that really counted. He had made a mistake letting Tez mentor East. Now he was going to fix it. If East showed any hesitation to follow his orders, Ricardo would know he could never trust him. It didn't matter how much he adored him. East would have to die along with Tez.

East took a deep breath. His stomach sunk, although his outer appearance remained unchanged. He had never killed anybody before. Now Ricardo was going to make him kill Tez as a test of his loyalty. He locked eyes with Dos hoping to find some type of support but found none. Dos refused to hold his gaze, turning his eyes away. They both knew who was responsible for the missing product. East had always followed his head and not his heart. The heart was just a motor. The head was meant to drive. At 20 years old, he thought he had it all mapped out. He would get what he could get out of the game and leave it alone. In and out, he told himself. He had always envisioned there would come a time, when he was set financially, that he could exit from the game. Now looking at Tez, a man twenty plus years his senior, he realized that would never happen. You didn't retire from the game, the game retired you, most times with a bullet.

Tez had lived his life governed by the same rules and honored the same codes he'd embedded in East, and where had it gotten him? Here. A young man who genuinely loved him was being forced to end his life. It was then that East realized what Tez had been mumbling under his breath the whole time, *"It wasn't me."*

East wondered how long Tez had tried to explain his side of the story to Ricardo. He thought Dos was a snake for placing blame on Tez. East also knew better to think Tez would ever beg for his life. He wasn't built like that. He was a gangster in every sense of the word. Right or wrong.

East took the gun out of Ricardo's hand and slowly walked behind Tez. He was stopped by the sound of Ricardo's commanding voice.

"Nah, not like that. In front, look a man in the eyes when you send him to God," he instructed. Ricardo didn't have a gun in his hand, but East knew he wouldn't leave the gym alive if he shot anyone besides Tez. That still didn't stop the thought from crossing his mind.

Just then Dos walked over, gun in hand. "Look up, fuck nigga," he taunted Tez. "Be a man about it."

East cocked his head and glared at Dos. "Fuckin' snake," he uttered under his breath. He felt that no matter what Tez was being accused of, he deserved more respect than he was being shown. Still, Tez didn't say anything and did as he was told. He looked up with not a tear in sight, staring directly at East.

When their eyes met, East could feel his heart wrench. He was consumed with emotions, causing him to hesitate for a moment. Ricardo was having none of it. He quickly nodded at Dos, who raised his gun, aiming it East's head.

"It's him or you, Eastwood," Ricardo stated, letting East know that if he didn't kill Tez, he would die also.

East eyed Dos intensely. He couldn't believe he was pointing a gun at him. Dos unsympathetically shrugged his shoulders, fully prepared to follow through on his father's orders. No matter what happened, after tonight their friendship would never be the same. East remained unfazed or afraid by what he was facing. His biggest flaw was his lack of fear. Whatever was coming his way, he would be a G about it.

"I'm sorry," Tez suddenly uttered. No one in the gym knew who his apology was meant for. Ricardo, East or God. Maybe it was meant for all three. East didn't want to know which, but in his heart told him it was for him.

East raised the gun pointing it at Tez's head. Tez had been the one that showed him how to use a gun. Both of them were sickened but grateful for the sight of one another on the opposite ends of the gun. If it had to be anybody, Tez was glad it was East. He had groomed him to be unflappable. Even now, his protégé's hand was steady as he felt the barrel of the gun press against his forehead. In a strange way, he found pride in that. He would be his first kill. Tez didn't move, blink or flinch. "Rule number 1?" he stated. The words caught East by surprise. Even in death Tez offered a lesson.

"Show no love," East whispered.

"Rule number 2?" Tez mumbled through the pain of his broken jaw.

"Trust no one." East forced himself to say as he fought back tears.

It was the last lesson Tez would ever remind East of but probably the most important. East squeezed the trigger. Tez's body flew backward off the stool, so hard that his knees made a cracking sound and his body made a thud as it hit the ground. Blood splatter smacking East in the face. The scent of Tez's blood in the air mixed with the smell of his shit. East felt a wave of calm wash over him, erasing the hesitation he had felt. Strangely, he felt nothing, no fear, no disgust, no anger. He had been trained to put bad things that happen out of his mind quickly.

Ricardo nodded to Dos who lowered his gun. He rubbed his beard as he approached. East had passed the test with flying colors. He was exactly who Ricardo thought he was. A no nonsense young nigga, all about his business with the heart to kill. He had a star pupil on his hands. "You did good, Eastwood," he said like a proud parent, grabbing East by the shoulders and shaking him. There was a joy in his voice that wasn't there before. "Your future is very bright, believe that," he proclaimed. Dos wasn't so happy. He didn't like his father openly doting on East all of a sudden.

East forced a smile and passed the gun back to Ricardo. Sure he was no longer in danger of being killed. He sneered at Dos. "You put a gun to my head. You should've pulled the trigger pussy."

"Fuck you. Next time I will," Dos barked.

"Won't be a next time," East assured him.

"Hey that's enough," Ricardo declared stepping

between them. "We're all family here."

East never responded. He took a final glance down at Tez's dead body, then walked out the backdoor of the gym. He got into a waiting car and Ricardo's men drove him home. East wasn't sad or even angry. For now, he was only numb, staring straight ahead in silence the whole ride.

CHAPTER FIFTEEN

Inside her small dorm room, Samayah sat Indian style on her bed with a laptop resting on her lap. Dressed in a FAMU hoodie and tights, her hair pulled up into a natural puff. Her brown skin was clear and freshly washed. Two large candles were filling the room with the scent of vanilla blossom as Lauryn Hill's voice flowed through her headphones. Textbooks, notepads, and pens were scattered across the bed as she studied.

A loud noise suddenly roared through the room like thunder. Samayah removed one of the headphones and focused her attention on the door. There was somebody knocking. Her face frowned up as she got up. *Why is somebody banging on my door*, she thought. She wasn't expecting company. She didn't know anybody on campus yet, only being there a few days.

"Who is it?" She asked as she unlocked the door. When she saw who was standing on the other side, her mouth dropped open. "East," she gasped, confused by his presence. Tallahassee was a long way from Miami. "What are you doing here? It's late. You trying to get me in trouble?" she asked in a hushed tone, looking over his shoulder nervously.

"I wasn't trying to do that. I just," he paused, shrugging his shoulders. "I got in my car and started driving, and somehow I ended up here," he admitted, lifting his eyes from the floor to meet hers.

Samayah saw the pain in his eyes. "What's wrong, East?"

He wanted to scream at the top of his lungs. Instead, he just stood there silent for a moment, then said, "Everything." It was like a weight being lifted off his chest. His answer told so little but so much at the same time. He didn't want to say too much, not because he didn't trust her. He did, more than anybody in the world probably. He just preferred to protect her from the truth of what he had done. Killing Tez had his head in a daze.

Still, his words worried her. "Everything? What

does that even mean?"

East stepped inside and she closed the door behind him. He cleared his throat and turned to face her. "It means, I heard you the other day. When you said, I needed to talk to somebody," he admitted as his chest swelled. He felt broken on the inside. He tried to continue but he couldn't find the words. He turned away from her, placing both hands on top of his head, fighting off tears. He took a deep breath to regain his composure then turned around. His jaw clenched tight as he held in his emotions. East swept a hand over his face. "I got a lot of pain pinned up inside of me. And I feel like it's gonna explode. I don't know what to do with it, Samayah. I don't what to do about it," he confessed. He was lost and he was begging her to help him find his way back.

She moved closer to him and caressed his face. "Share it with me." If she could've merged her heart with his, she would've done it at that very moment. Just to take away the pain, she would've endured it, if he didn't have to hurt anymore.

East rested his head on her forehead and found himself lost in her eyes. Their amber hue still held innocence in them. He stared at her with so much admiration. There was so much that needed to be said but suddenly neither could find their voice. Just the fact that he was there was enough for Samayah. She didn't care about the trouble she could get in. She would risk everything she had so hard worked for, for him. There was no way she would tell him no. He needed her and she had waited a lifetime to be needed by him.

Since she was 11 years old, he had been her weakness. Now she would be his strength. *For a man to drive 6 hours for a shoulder to cry on, he had to be in drowning in pain*, she thought to herself.

East couldn't breathe. The mixture of anger and sadness had a death grip on him. Tears clouded his vision. "I should've been there. I should've known. I could've saved her," he whispered. He didn't have to say *her* name, for Samayah to know he meant his mother, Ebony.

"It's ok," she said in a comforting tone. She hurt for him but knew it could never compare to what he was feeling. She couldn't imagine such pain.

"How could she be so selfish?" East gritted his teeth. He couldn't hide his anger. It was all spilling out for Samayah to see. He had buried it long enough, pretending not to feel anything. Pretending everything was fine, when it wasn't.

"You have to go see her, East," she pleaded with him.

"No," he protested, shaking his head like a child disobeying a parent.

"You have to forgive her."

"I can't," he whispered as tears rolled down his face. He hadn't. He was still enraged. That's why he hadn't been to her gravesite. He couldn't bring himself to go see her. He resented his mother for what she had done.

Samayah wiped his tears and held his face in her hand. "You have to, for yourself. You gotta let go of that animosity. So, you can move on with your life. If not, you'll always be a prisoner to it." The hatred was radiating from him. She could feel it all in his energy. It was eating away at him. Destroying the person, she knew him to be.

East turned and walked away from her. "I did something last night. Something that I can't undo."

Samayah stared at his back. She hesitated to speak, allowing his words to linger in the air. She felt nervous, unsure if she wanted to know what that something was. Her eyes filled with a hint of sadness and heart with a bit of fear. Fear of losing him to the streets like she had lost her brother to jail.

He turned and saw the concern on her face. He walked over to her. So now they were face to face. "You see why it isn't a good idea for us to be together?

I'm a street nigga. That comes with a lifestyle you don't have to subject yourself to. You got options, ma. I'm not one of them."

"Then why are you here?" she whispered softly. Something in her soul was drawn to him. She had watched him mature from a humble young boy to an honorable man. *The man she loved,* she thought as she stood there staring at him like she saw heaven in his eyes. Samayah wanted him off her mind and on her body.

East ran his hand over her hair, smoothing out her ponytail in the most affectionate way then down her face. She was the epitome of beauty. Even with no makeup on. Her flawless skin, doe eyes and smile were all she'd ever needed to impress him. Samayah's body ached in pleasure when he touched her. Both of their foreheads were together as he spoke to her, "Because this is where I belong."

She kept her eyes closed as she took in his words and intoxicating smell. The hint of Hennessy on his breath was inviting and she wanted to taste him. His aura commanded her attention and awoke her body. He kissed her lips. She welcomed it, pressed her face against his and slipped her tongue into his mouth. East engulfed her in his arms. He held on to her with everything in him, like he was trying to absorb her into his body. She melted into his embrace. His strong arms around her, comforting her, made her feel safe. When she looked at East, she didn't see a hood nigga, she saw a king. One she didn't mind standing beside.

In one swift motion, East lifted her off the ground her feet and sat on the bed, allowing her to straddle him. She felt light as a feather on a natural high. She wrapped her arms around his neck and grazed her manicure tips across his neck. Jolts of electricity ran up East's spine. He inhaled her scent into his being and she did the same.

Samayah could feel his hard dick pressing against her and suddenly became nervous. *It was really happening,* she thought in her mind. "I've never did this before," she uttered.

"Me either," he replied then smiled with boyish charm at the shook look on her face. "I'm just playing. Relax, I got you. Don't worry."

"Ok," she whispered in a sexy tone. She wanted to submit to him.

That was all East needed to hear. He pulled her hoodie over her head and tossed it aside. Samayah stood up and removed her tights. East removed his clothes. His dick swelling in anticipation when he took in a full view of her naked body. She was perfect.

The seductive look on her face turned him on more. She sought his approval. He nodded his head, more in admiration than acceptance. He pulled her to him and kissed on her stomach then trailed kisses down to her shaved pussy. East lifted one of her legs, letting it rest on one of his broad shoulders. Then Snaked his tongue in places she had no idea could feel like that when licked. Palming her ass as he pushed his face into her middle, flicking his tongue on her clit bring it alive. Samayah moaned, arching her back. She grinded, snaking her hips on his face while rubbing his head. East devoured her virgin sweetness. He couldn't get enough, eating her pussy like he had been starved of it all his life.

"You taste so good ma," he whispered. East wrapped his full lips around her clit and sucked. Applying just the right amount of pressure to her pearl. It drove Samayah wild. Her eyes squeezing shut, her head fell back as she cried out in pleasure.

"Oh God, what are you doing to me?" she moaned feeling her orgasm building. The feeling was so intense that it frightened her. "What's happening to me?" she panicked as her legs wobbled. "East, why do I feel like this?" she panted nervously.

"Shhh, just enjoy it ma," he instructed smoothly, gripping her ass tighter, burying his face into her, sucking faster and faster until her orgasm exploded.

"Oh God, East!" she called out, losing all control of her body. She thought she was having a seizure. Her toes curled as she trembled uncontrollably. It was unlike anything she had ever felt. Better than she could have ever imagined. East held her firm to keep her from falling.

He placed her down on the bed then reached in his pocket and retrieved a condom. He tore it open with his mouth then placed it on his rock-hard dick. He pulled himself up until he was hovering over her with his arms locked. Samayah eyes were still shut.

"Look at me," he demanded softly.

"I can't," she whined. "I can't open my eyes," she confessed. Her chest heaving up and down as her body quivered.

East smirked. "Look at me, ma," he repeated as he slowly eased his girth inside of her wetness. He knew he was crossing the point of no return once he entered her body. He no longer cared. Samayah opened her eyes and gripped his arms, digging her nails into him as he filled her walls completely. When their eyes met East spoke again, "Relax. I got you," he reminded her in a loving tone.

He began giving her slow steady strokes in and out of her pussy. Samayah's moans grew louder with every entry, panting every time he exited her. East took his time pleasing her. Every stroke was delivered precise and intense. His mouth slightly ajar, loving the tightness of her pussy.

"That feels so good," Samayah moaned her approval. He didn't ever have to ask. She was trying to control her screams, but East would have none of it.

"Don't hold back. Let it out," he commanded, each word was accompanied by a slow deep stroke. "This is mine now, you understand? Never give my pussy away to nobody else. You hear me?"

"Yes," she moaned, becoming wetter and wetter. Her juices pouring over his dick effortlessly. Her mouth fell open in an O of pleasure. East was hitting spots she never knew existed. She thought her stomach shifted every time he pumped. She clawed at his tattooed back, inviting him deep inside.

"I don't believe you," he responded, grabbing her arms and pinning them down. "Make me believe you," he demanded, stroking deeper inside of her.

"Yes! Yes!" Samayah screamed with pleasure.

"Yes, what?".

"Yes. This is your pussy East," she declared.

"And you'll never give it away?"

"I'll never give it away," she repeated after him.

"Say that shit then. Say it like you mean it," he commanded. His thrust becoming stronger as his climax built.

"It's yours baby. I promise. I'll never give it to anybody else."

When they locked eyes, East stared deep into hers. He placed his hand under her chin. "Do you love me ma?" he bit down on his lip then kissed her.

For Samayah, time stopped, at that moment, they were the only two people on earth. "Yes. I love you, East" she wept tears of pleasure and pain, both with pure satisfaction as she pledged her heart and body to him. "I love you," she repeated over and over as she climaxed.

"I love you too," East groaned. He felt his climax and started stroking her harder until he could no longer contain his eruption.

As they laid next to each other, Samayah sighed with bliss. Her heart was pounding in her chest. East ran his fingers through her hair as his chest heaved up and down. Their bodies still tingling from head to toe.

PART IV: RESPECT THE GAME

CHAPTER SIXTEEN:
EIGHT MONTHS
LATER

East pulled his black '66 Chevy Impala into the Annie Coleman housing projects in Liberty City. Since the night of Tez's murder, the dynamics of his relationship with Ricardo had changed. He was no longer hired muscle, protecting Lauryn. Now Ricardo was supplying him with product, and he was flourishing. East and Dos was another story. They remained at odds. Their relationship permanently damaged by the events of that night.

Still, East was doing well for himself, controlling a few spots of his own. This one was inside the projects, known as The Rockies, that was making about $5,500 a day. He needed a three-man team to run the spot, making sure everything went smoothly. East was big on loyalty, so naturally he chose Que and his friend Sameer, who recently had been released from jail. They had all came up together like a family. Sameer had recommended a solid young nigga from Carol City named Flaco, that he had been locked up with as the third man. If Sameer vouched for him, that was good enough for East. He turned out to be everything Sameer said he was. The three of them had no problem playing their position. They all understood that gunplay was part of the game. East made sure his team stayed fully loaded and instilled in them to play no games whatsoever. On more than one occasion, they had to put in gun work to defend the turf.

East grabbed the bag from under his seat then slid the Glock .40 in his waist. He checked his surroundings before getting out the car. There was a lot of foot traffic moving up and down the street. The courtyard was lined with junkies. East made his way through them all, his chain swinging back and forth on his shirt, walking up to the apartment on the second floor. Things seemed to be moving the way he liked it. He made sure his spots never ran out of work. East knocked on the door and immediately heard barking coming from the other side. A few seconds later, Sameer opened the door and let him in. "What up, Screw?"

"What's up, Woe?" he replied slapping five with his comrade then shutting the door. He was holding a vicious Pitbull at bay on a leash. "Sit," he instructed the dog and it did. Sameer's body had filled out while he was gone. He was still tall, standing 6'3, and handsome, but his slim frame was filled out with muscle. He sported a thick beard. He was covered in tattoos, a rose with his mother's name covering his throat the most prominent. His hair was long and curly. He usually wore it out but today in was in four thick cornrows. His pants sagged off his ass exposing a gun on his waistline. At 19, he was a year younger than East but inch taller and a lot wilder.

"What up nigga? You always stuffing your fuckin' face," East joked to Que, who was sitting on a fold up chair feasting on some Jerk Chicken, Rice and Peas. Que nodded in agreement and smiled. His boyish good looks and dimples on full display. At 18, he was the baby of the bunch. He was stocky built, had a butter scotch complexion with slanted eyes and was arrogantly funny.

The small apartment that they were trapping out of had nothing more in it than a couch, a TV with a video game hooked to it, a table with weed on it and a chopper laying across the couch where Screw had been sitting.

"How's this shit movin'?" East asked, sitting the bag on the table.

"Faster than a muthafucka. We'll probably be done with dat there in a few hours," Screw said confidently.

"Yeah, money coming through here faster than we can count the shit," Que added while licking the tips of his fingers.

"For real?" East questioned like he didn't believe what he was hearing. Although, he knew he was getting the best coke in the city from Ricardo.

"This shit that A1 pedico." Screw boasted. "The J's loving it. We just made fifteen hundid in a half hour." A knock on the door grabbed their attention and made the dog start barking again. It was a sell and another one followed right behind it.

"Where the boy Flaco?" East looked around, noticing he was missing.

"He made a store run. We out of baggies."

The sound of the toilet flushing grabbed East's attention. He turned in the direction of the bathroom. "I know y'all niggas ain't got no bitches in here?" he barked. Clearly not feeling the idea of them having some females from the projects in the trap spot.

"Nigga, that's Twin," Screw dismissed. "She brought us some food. We ain't ate shit all day," he continued to explain.

Seconds later, Samayah emerged from the bathroom, wearing a black lounger jumpsuit and heels. She had big hoop earrings in her ears and a black and gold, mini Chanel bag in her hand. Her hair was up in a bun. Her eyebrows were perfectly arched and her nails freshly manicured.

East's brow bent when their eyes met. The fact that she was looking so damn good did nothing to melt his icy glare. He noticed it but his first thought was, *What the hell was she doing there?* He looked over at Screw and Que. "I don't want nobody in the spot. I'on care who it is. This ain't no hangout."

"Hello to you too," Samayah huffed. "I just had to use the bathroom. I wasn't staying long," she spoke up, sucking her teeth, "Just give me the money for Mama so I can go," she told her brother sticking out her hand.

East didn't say another word but all in the room could see he was still angry. Screw dug in his pocket and pulled out a knot of money. He passed his sister two crisp $100 dollar bills. "Tell Mama, I love her," he said.

"You need to go tell her yourself. She said, she hasn't seen you in a week," she said, stuffing the money in her handbag.

"Yeah, I know," he admitted then kissed her on the cheek. Samayah left without saying goodbye to anyone else. Screw turned to East after shutting the door behind her, "My fault, Moms needed—"

East lifted his hand and cut him off. "You ain't gotta apologize for shit. Moms always come first. I understand," he said." It had been more than two years since his mother's death. Not a day went by that she didn't cross his mind. Although he still hadn't brought himself to go see her. He just wasn't there yet. Ms. Ang had become like a second mother to him in Ebony's absence. Just the mention of her made East's angry stare disappear. "Yall got that bread for me?" he asked rubbing his hands together, getting right back to the business.

"Is a pig's pussy pork?" Que replied and rose from the chair. He sat his food on the counter before entering the kitchen. Reaching inside one of the cabinets, he pulled out a plastic shopping bag that was full of rubber band stacks of money. He walked over to East and handed it to him. "We gone sell out before the morning tho. I'm telling you."

"Y'all should be good with that," East assured him, pointing to the bag on the table. It contained enough coke for the spot to run for at least another 24 hours. He never kept more dope in the spot than needed. That way if police raided or the spot got robbed, he wouldn't take a big loss.

He looked down at his phone. He had a text message. He read it to himself then looked back up at Screw. "I'ma need you to ride with me to go see Ricardo tomorrow."

"Bet," Screw said. He knew that meant East was going to re-up and needed an extra set of eyes and gun with him. Screw was East's right hand. The one he trusted more than anybody because he never hesitated to swing his iron in a tight spot.

A knock at the door made the dog bark again. They all paused. Screw walked to the door with the gun in hand. He relaxed when he saw Flaco through the peephole. "Here this nigga Waka Flacka go right here," he said.

Flaco stepped inside. His pants sagged low, damn near showing his whole ass. He smiled, showing all the gold slugs in his mouth when he spotted East. "I thought I seen that old school out there," he greeted, giving him a pound. Flaco's name came from his slender build. He had a dark complexion with long, matted dreads he wore banded together. He was unmistakably Dade County born and raised.

"What up, homie? East replied. "I'm in and out."

"We know you move like a ghost, nigga," Flaco joked.

East gave his three comrades dap then left the spot. He headed a few blocks away to an apartment he used as a stash house. Once inside, he put up the money he had collected. Minutes later, he was back in his car, on the move again, heading straight to Miami Gardens.

Pulling into the parking lot of Miami Finga Licking, East parked next to a car with the engine running. He rolled his window down and simultaneously, the passenger side window of the other car did as well.

"What took you so long?" Samayah said as she looked over at him. "You act like somebody got all day to be waiting on you," she teased then smiled.

East didn't smile. "Why you ain't leave then?" he asked confidently. "You wanted something out of here?" he pointed towards the restaurant. When she lifted a bag with takeout, he nodded.

She got out the car and got in with him, waving to her homegirl as they pulled away. East stared in the rearview mirror back at the car she had gotten out of. There was a female in the driver seat. Samayah saw the look on his face and tried to put his mind at ease.

"Don't worry. That's my friend from school. She's not gonna run her mouth. She doesn't know you or my brother," she explained. Out of respect, they were still keeping their thing a secret.

East ran his hand over the light beard on his face. "Who said I was worried?" he said evenly. "What are you doing home?" He cut straight to it. "Why you not at school?" He looked her up and down.

"Oh, since we're asking question. Why haven't I seen you in two weeks," she sassed.

"Oh, so that's what you doing? Getting all dressed up and popping up on me. That's why you were at the trap?"

"Yes," she didn't lie. "I knew you would be there," she said.

"You gotta relax, ma. You know for somebody so smart, that was dumb," East said. "It's not safe for you to be there. You know that. I been handling business. That's why I haven't been up to see you the past two weeks. I call you every night, tho. And when I spoke to you last night, you ain't say nothing about coming home," he eyed her suspiciously.

Samayah gave him a mischievous smile. "I

missed you," she confessed, kissing him on the cheek, trying to butter him up. "I got you some food?" she said like a childlike voice.

"I don't care, you're still taking your ass right back to school tomorrow." They both laughed.

"I don't care, a girl got needs." East knew exactly how to fulfil her needs. He was too sexy to deny herself the pleasure. The sexual chemistry between them was unmatched. It wasn't all about sex with them, even though they had plenty. They loved each other.

"I brought you something?" Samayah announced.

"You didn't have to do that." He told her.

"Yes, I did." She reached in her bag, pulled out a book and handed it to him.

"A book?" he questioned.

"Look at it?" she pleaded.

East looked down at the book. "No Time to Say Goodbye," he read the title aloud.

"It's about surviving the suicide of a loved one," she explained.

East got quiet. His silence made her second guess the gift. *Maybe I shouldn't have*, she thought. "I'm sorry. I was only trying to help."

"I know. It's just," he hesitated before continuing,

"Nobody ever did nothing like that for me. It means a lot. Thank you. I love you," he flashed a charming smile. His pearly white teeth only enhanced his handsome face. It made her smile back.

"Aww babe, I love you too," Samayah was so happy. They kissed, first passionately then lustfully.

But by the time they arrived at the hotel room on Biscayne Boulevard, the lust between them was on full display. East sat on the edge of the bed with no shirt and a pair of boxer briefs. He had the build of an athlete, standing 6'2, solid without being overly muscular. His arms, back and chest were covered with tattoos that popped off his honey dipped skin.

Samayah approached and stood between his legs, wearing nothing but a red bra and panties. She was super thick in all the right places, beautiful with a feisty edge hidden beneath the surface. Her body sported a new tattoo, her first. A bouquet of thorn stem roses that ran down her side. East ran his hand over the artwork.

"You like it," she asked.

"Love it."

A smile spread across her face as she caressed his head, rubbing her hand over his waves. East's naturally slanted eyes were even lower from the weed they were smoking. He took a long pull,

Samayah leaned in and he blew the smoke into her mouth. Their lips met as he palmed her ass. He could hear the wetness of her pussy as he spread her ass cheeks. He slid her panties to the side and rubbed her clit. He passed her the weed, she hit it twice then passed it back. Samayah blew the smoke into the air then got down on her knees, pulling East's manhood out of his boxer briefs. He had length and girth. His dick felt heavy in her hand. She began to stroke it. Looking seductively into his eyes. She circled her tongue around the mushroom shaped tip then slid his full erection into her warm, wet mouth. East hit the weed and watched as her head bobbed up and down, making his dick disappear then reappear. His head fell back as she took him deeper into her throat, wet sounds and slurps filling the room. He blew a cloud of smoke from his lungs, then ashed the weed.

"Damn ma," he grunted. He couldn't take it any longer. When Samayah came up for air, he pulled her up to her feet then down on top of him aggressively. She straddled him, sliding down on him, letting out a soft moan as she took him deep inside her. Her eyes rolled into the back of her head as his thickness filled her. She exploded instantly.

"Oh shit," Samayah moaned as she held on to his broad shoulders and bounced up and down. He gripped her ass cheeks, digging deep in her pussy with long strokes. She could feel the pressure in her stomach. They were both breathing heavy, kissing one another passionately as their bodies became one. The synchrony between their bodies made the sex look like performance art. East grabbed her by the throat and applied pressure. He just wanted her pleasure and she just wanted his pain. "I fuckin' missed you," she called out as her mouth fell open in orgasmic bliss.

"I missed you too."

"I love you," she whispered. He felt so good inside of her.

* * *

Dos stood on the balcony of his luxury condo overlooking Biscayne Bay with his phone to his ear. From his high perch, he had a perfect view of the water and American Airlines Arena in the distance. His night had been going similar to his view, until it was interrupted by a phone call.

"I ain't tryin' hear that shit right now, Jaz," he barked into the phone. "It ain't like you didn't know from day one what it was. I told you I wasn't shit. I told you not to fall in love with me. You chose not to listen. Now here we are."

"That's not fair," Jasmine sobbed on the other

end of the phone.

"Life's not always fair, ma," Dos said coldly.

"What about our son?" she tried using the one thing she knew he cared about. She had given him what every man dreamed of; a male heir. Someone to carry on his legacy after he was gone. The only thing was Dos was still building his legacy. In his mind, he had only just begun.

"I love my son," he proclaimed truthfully.

"Just not me...right?" Jasmine asked as the phone went silent. She truly loved Dos, despite all the shit he had put her through. The different women. The constant cheating. She had stayed through it all. He was the father of her child. She just wanted them to be a family.

Dos was the sky to her, a respected dope boy with a dope dick and money to burn. She was hooked. There was only one problem, Dos wasn't trying to be tied down to one woman, baby mother or not. He was the prince of the city and he couldn't wait to be king. He changed women like he did his underwear, and he showered twice a day. His heart was filled with ambition, that's it. There wasn't any room for love. By the time Jasmine realized it, she was already too deep in love with a baby on the way.

"I ain't tryin' go back and forth about this shit all

night. I got shit to do," he declared.

"I love you, Dos. Just come home so we can talk," she pleaded with him.

"Home?" he laughed into the phone then hung up.

Jasmine lay in bed, holding her son on her chest. She was a thousand miles away from her entire family back in Queens. She felt more alone than ever. Her son was all she had left. She closed her eyes, feeling the tears escape out the sides. Her heartbeat increased as she cried in silence, not wanting her son to hear her grief. She kissed him on the forehead as he slept peacefully in her arms. Jasmine made a promise to herself that she would raise him to be nothing like the man that had helped make him. She kissed him again then placed him down on the bed next to her as tears continued to spill down her cheeks. She rose from the bed, grabbing the rolled up weed off the nightstand in one motion. She needed to smoke one to calm her nerves. She walked out onto the balcony of her luxury apartment with nothing on but a small T-shirt and high waist thong panties. Her brown, round ass cheeks hung out the bottom of her panties as she strutted across the room. Dos had her living in the heart of the Brickell District in downtown Miami. Surrounded by fine dining and boutiques, where she could shop as much as she wanted to. He had provided her with the best of everything, from fashion to jewelry. She could have anything her heart desired, but it didn't matter. The material things meant nothing now. What her heart desired the most was him. The one thing she couldn't have the way she wanted. She would trade all the luxuries afforded to her, just to be with the man she loved. She would give anything to have Dos sleeping next to her every night. Making love to her body. The thought of Dos touching her body made Jasmine shut her eyes, briefly relive one of their many nights of passionate sex. With her looks, she could bed any man she wanted but she only wanted Dos and wouldn't dare cheat on him. Even if he didn't believe her when she told him so. He would just laugh in her face. Instead of believing and appreciating her, Dos would keep his distance for weeks at a time, popped in to fuck then he would be gone again.

As Jasmine stood overlooking downtown Miami, she felt like she was mourning death. That's how much it hurt. She was devastated, heartbroken and confused, unable to grasp any of her thoughts. Her heart was so heavy in her chest, she could barely breathe. The weight of her emotions seemed too much to bear on her body. She felt stupid for loving him. She looked over her shoulder, back at her son laying on the bed. Her heart nearly broke in two. What was she supposed to do now? How did she go forward? Without Dos, she had no idea of what would become of her and her child. The thought alone caused her to lose what was left of her composure. Her heart wrenched. She began crying hysterically, snot and tears making a mess of her pretty face. She was in the midst of a storm. One she didn't know if she could weather. "Everything was falling apart," she whispered. "But we're gonna to be alright," she told herself, looking back at her son who was the spitting image of Dos. She had to muster the strength to survive for him, even if she couldn't do it for herself.

Jasmine lit the backwood, took a long pull then exhaled deeply. She began wiping away the tears on her face. Dos had committed one of the deadliest sins known to a woman; betrayal. There was nothing more dangerous than a woman scorned. "This nigga done broke my heart for the last time," she seethed out loud trying to convince herself. Hatred burning in her soul. Suddenly, those watery eyes became steely ones. Her broken heart became black as it beat violently in her chest. She wanted Dos to hurt like she did.

Back inside Dos' condo, Jasmine was the furthest

thing from his mind. A thick redbone stripper with blonde hair was ass naked and hunched over the table sniffing lines of cocaine through a hundred-dollar bill. Coke wasn't Dos' thing, he only smoked weed but he didn't have a problem providing the party favors. Another badass, Cuban stripper was lying across the couch ass naked as well. She was high off coke, feeling hot and horny. They had all just finished fucking and she was ready for another round.

"Ven aqui papi," she said with a cute Spanish accent. "Let me suck that big dick." She licked her lips.

Dos smiled and walked towards the couch. He was already hard. He stood in front of her as she slid to the edge of the couch and grabbed his dick aggressively. Dos rubbed his hand through her long, silky hair as she smacked herself in the face with his manhood. She began to suck on his balls as the redbone with the blonde hair joined in, playing with the tip of his dick with her tongue. They alternated, one sucking his dick, the other licking his balls. Dos put both hands behind her head and leaned his head back with his eyes closed. All he could hear was wet and popping sounds as they went to work. Finally, the redbone looked up at him and said, "Fuck me, daddy."

"You want this dick, bitch?" he said, aggressively bending her over the arm of the couch with her ass up in the air.

"Fuck this pussy," she purred, looking over her shoulder at him.

Dos smacked her fat ass and grabbed her hips as he entered her from the back.

"Yes," she moaned, throwing her ass back at him. "Deeper daddy, deeper."

Dos began punishing her, digging in her guts harder. Her ass jiggled and rippled like waves in the ocean as she received every thrust. "Oh my God," she began to scream at the top of her lungs, from the intense orgasm. Dos continued pounding until the other stripper became jealous.

"Bring that dick over here, papi," she moaned out to him. Her legs were spread, up in the air like a peace sign and she was rubbing her clit.

Dos walked over and plunged his rock-hard manhood into her wet pussy. She started to cum instantly, biting down on her lip and caressing her own breast. "Oh yes, like that, papi, I love it," she cried out from the pleasure.

"I know you do," he bragged.

"Fuck that tight little pussy," the redbone shouted

instructions as she rubbed her clit and looked on.

Dos' stroke became more powerful and deliberate as he felt his climax nearing. He clenched his teeth and pumped harder and harder.

"Yeah, baby give me that nut," the redbone called out to him.

Dos pulled out of the Cuban stripper and released his seed all over the redbone beauty's face. "Ahhh," he grunted then collapsed on to the couch breathing heavily.

CHAPTER
SEVENTEEN

Watching from the ground as his shooter fled on foot, Ricardo could feel the warmth of his own blood beneath him. He felt a searing pain in his body like he had never felt before. It had all happened so fast. The assassin appeared out of thin air. Ricardo hadn't even heard the first shot, but he felt it and the slugs that followed. The fact that he was in so much pain, was the only reason he knew he was still alive. *But for how long?* He needed medical attention immediately. But it was so early in the morning that no one was around. Searching the alley, he couldn't understand why his bodyguards hadn't come to his aid yet. Then he spotted their dead bodies stretched out a few feet away. Ricardo tried to move but he couldn't find the strength to drag his body into the backdoor of his gym. He lay there staring up at the cloudy grey sky, clinging to life with thoughts of his past playing in his mind. With every breath he took, another ghost would appear to him, friends and foes alike. There were so many faces that they started to blur together and so did his vision. He could feel his strength waning then darkness and silence engulfed him.

The ambulance's siren pierced the air like the wail of a woman in agony as it raced along the rain slicked streets. Pedestrians and drivers alike watched as it whizzed by with looks of apprehension on their faces. It was like they could feel the impending drama building in the air, because many of them already knew who was inside. The shooting had only occurred a short time ago, but the streets were already abuzz with what had gone down. Ricardo Wheeler had been shot outside his boxing gym. Both of his trusted bodyguards had been killed in the process. Talk was rampant in the streets as to who was responsible. No one knew but what was known was that in the streets of Miami, some dudes were respected, some were feared, and some were loved. Ricardo was all three.

* * *

The black Ford F150 pulled alongside a ran down Honda in the secluded spot behind an abandoned church. Kev quickly jumped out and got into Rio's truck.

"Put the gun in there, he said immediately passing Kev a small, black lockbox. "I gotta make that shit disappear ASAP.

Kev placed the gun in the box, he still was breathing heavily from the rush of adrenaline.

"You got him?" Rio asked.

"Hell yeah," Kev answered like he had been offended. "You ain't dealin wit' an amateur," he bragged. "I hit him and the two niggas wit 'em at least three, four times each. Left them all slumped in the parking lot."

"Are you sure he's dead?" Rio pressed. He was dead serious. He turned his body to face Kev wanting to see his eyes when he answered.

"Yeah, nigga. He dead as shit," Kev assured him. The fact the Rio was pressing him so hard made him a little annoyed. Kev was ready to get paid and get gone. "Where's the bricks you promised?"

Rio could sense the urgency within the truck too. "They're in the backseat," he said, pointing.

That's all Kev wanted to hear. His eyes lit up as he reached in the back and grabbed the back. He unzipped it with excitement in his eyes, but his expression quickly changed when he didn't see anything inside. "It ain't shit in here—"

With a noise no louder than a whisper, Rio filled Kev's body with four shots from a gun with a silencer. Kev's body slowly leaned against the door of the truck. Rio reached across his body and opened it, letting Kev's body fall to the ground. Rio had never planned on letting Kev live. He was just a means to an end. He knew too much and Rio didn't trust him enough to believe he could keep a secret. The less people that knew the truth about Ricardo's murder the better. The only thing was Ricardo wasn't dead, at least not yet.

* * *

East was awake in the bed next to a still sleeping Samayah. He was trying to force himself not to think about his mother or Tez. Not a day had past that he didn't miss them both or regret killing Tez. East had been taught to quickly put things out his mind. It was a skill that had served him well up until now. But killing Tez was the one thing he couldn't shake. And his mother committing suicide was the one thing he couldn't forgive. It had continued to bother him. The pain hadn't faded over the years, it only seemed to increase. Nothing had felt the same since he lost both of them. A piece of him had died along with them. He rolled over and grabbed the book Samayah had gifted him off the nightstand. He stared at the cover then opened it to the first page. Suddenly, his phone rang on the nightstand, interrupting him.

"What's up bro?" he quickly answered, thankful for the distraction. "I'll be by to get you in about an hour so we can go handle that," he said.

"Nah. That's not why I'm calling. You see the news?" Screw asked.

"Nah, what's up?"

Screw was animated, "Nigga, turn on the news, right now."

"Hold up," East sat up and grabbed the remote, turning on the TV. There was breaking news. A deadly shooting. Two dead bodies covered with sheets, in front of Ricardo's boxing gym.

"Somebody tried to kill Ricardo," Screw said.

East rose from the bed with such urgency that it woke Samayah.

"What's wrong?" she said in a fog of sleepiness, her heart pounding from being startled.

"Let me call you back," East quickly rushed to hang up the phone, not wanting Screw to recognize his sister's voice. He told himself that this sneaking around shit had to end. He had to be the one to bring it to the forefront because he knew she never would. They were in love. It was what it was. Screw and Ms. Ang would have to understand. Whatever it was going to be, it was going to be. He was tired of keeping it a secret.

"What's going on?" Samayah asked, her naked body peeking from under the sheets.

East didn't respond immediately. Not out of rudeness but he didn't have an answer. He used the remote to increase the volume and they both listened to the female reporter on the TV. She hadn't even finished her report before he was getting dressed.

"What's happening?" the concern in Samayah's voice was evident.

It served as another reminder to East why she needed to be back on campus. She needed to be as far away from shit like this as possible. He would lose his mind if something was to happen to her. He wouldn't forgive himself for ruining her future.

"Isn't that Ricardo's gym on—"

East interrupted her before she could finish her sentence. "Yeah," he said solemnly. "Somebody shot him."

"Is he dead?" Samayah covered her mouth in shock.

"I don't know but I gotta get to the hospital. Get

dressed," he instructed. I gotta take you...home," The last words coming out a bit awkward.

"You can drop me at my girl's house, I call her on the way," Samayah told him, then smirked at the look of relief his face showed. She slid off the bed and kissed him.

* * *

The loud banging at the door, startled Dos from his sleep. He removed the legs of the naked women in his bed from across his body, grabbed his gun from under his pillow and got out the bed.

"Dos! Dos wake up! Open the door! get up!" the voice screamed on a continuous loop from the other side of the door.

Dos looked through the peephole. His cousin Rio was on the other side with a frantic look on his face. Dos snatched the door open and stood in the doorway naked with his gun in his hand. "What the fuck is wrong with you, nigga? You high?" he asked with a scowl on his face.

"It's Unc," Rio said. "He got shot outside the gym this morning. He still alive but..."

Dos didn't even stand there long enough to let his cousin finish his sentence. He raced to grab some clothes.

* * *

The doors of the emergency room opened, East turned in time to see Dos marching through them, dressed in a Nike jogging suit with Rio following close behind. His chest heaved up and down as he stormed over to the nurse's station. "I need to see my father," he barked, banging his hands down on the desk. He was full of adrenaline and could barely contain his anger. Dos always operated purely off emotions.

The security guard on duty quickly approached. "Sir, you're gonna have to calm down or I'ma have to ask you to leave," his voice boomed through the ER.

Dos pinched the tip of his nose and looked up at the ceiling. "My father was just shot. If you don't wanna be next, you'll get the fuck outta my face," he threatened the security guard. The cold stare made the man take a step back. Dos was heated that the security guard would have the audacity to press him.

Rio stepped in and walked the security guard away, trying to smooth the situation over.

"Sir, please calm down. So, I can help you," one of the older nurses spoke up, trying to defuse the situation with Dos. She had a soothing voice and seemed to be the one in charge.

"I'm calm," Dos replied. His chest still heaving up and down.

"Now what is your father's name, young man? And when was he brought—"

Before the nurse could finish her questions, Dos turned and saw East quickly approaching them for across the lobby. He met him halfway. Without greeting he asked, "Where's my father?"

East shrugged his shoulders. "I don't know, they wouldn't tell me nothing either."

Dos sighed in frustration. "What are you doing here anyway?" he scoffed. There was distaste in his tone.

"Same thing you're doing here," East retorted.

Dos chuckled inwardly. They had once been close but that was no longer the case. Dos viewed East as beneath him. Truth was, East wasn't born to follow. He had boss potential. Ricardo knew it and so did Dos deep down inside.

"Excuse me nurse," the sultry sound of a woman's voice called out. "I'm Mrs. Wheeler. Can you tell me where my husband is?"

East and Dos turned towards Lauryn, who was standing at the nurse's station, flanked by two bodyguards. Nearly a decade younger than her husband, Lauryn mesmerized any man that looked at her. She had unmatched beauty with flawless bronze skin and a tight body. You would have sworn by her attire that she had rushed there from the gym. She wore a vintage 2Pac graphic t-shirt and black tight with a pair of Air Max 270 on her feet. But hair gave it away. It was perfectly twisted into long faux locs that hung to one side. That along with the Hermes Birkin handbag she toted, the spoils of being the trophy wife of a boss. It was clear that she hadn't come from Planet Fitness working up a sweat. She had dry tear lines on her face. Her eyes were red and swollen from crying the whole ride to the hospital.

"Here comes the doctor now ma'am. He will be able to tell you everything you need to know." the nurse pointed in the direction of a tall, slender white man in a white lab coat.

Lauryn rushed over to the him with Dos, East and Rio right behind her. "Doctor, I'm Mrs. Wheeler, is my husband okay?" She didn't realize that she was holding her breath, bracing for his answer.

The doctor was caught off guard by the sight of the beautiful women standing in front of him. She looked more like his patient's daughter than his wife. He cleared his throat to regain his professionalism, preparing to deliver the news. "Well ma'am, your husband's condition is still very touch and go at this moment. He was shot multiple times. We are doing everything we can for him."

Tears blinded her eyes as they ran down her face. She shook her head. Her legs felt weak. Her emotions were all over the place. She grabbed the doctor's arm. "Can I see him, please? Just for a minute." She eyed the doctor with her soft brown eyes that made men melt. The doctor was no exception.

He cleared his throat once again as his face became a blushing red. "I'm sorry Mrs. Wheeler, did you say it was? I wish I could, but I have to say no. It's too early," he answered before trying to walk away.

Dos grabbed the doctor's arm, stopping him in his tracks. He squeezed so tight the doctor could feel the circulation stop. Dos stepped closer, so now their faces were only inches apart. "My father better live or you won't, understand me?" he threatened the doctor. The crazed look in his eyes struck fear in the poor man.

"Dos chill," Rio said, grabbing his arm, trying to calm the escalating tension. "That ain't helping the situation. Let the man do his job."

East exhaled deeply and shook his head.

Dos released the doctor's arm then shot Rio a menacing look. Rio let his arm go. Dos eyed East for a moment then walked away in anger. The bodyguard that had accompanied Lauryn escorted her to the waiting room. Suddenly, Dos stopped midstride and marched back over to East. "Let me holla at you outside," East nodded and with that, they headed for the front door.

Once they were outside, Rio stayed back while Dos and East walked side by side. Dos lit a Newport and took a long drag. He was on edge. "Where you were this morning?"

East laughed. "What you trying to say?"

"You hard of hearing? I said where were you this morning, when my father got shot? Cuz you been acting different ever since that night with Tez. Now you up here at the hospital, acting all concerned and shit, it don't add up," Dos anger was at a rolling boil.

"Nigga, you don't even believe that shit, you're saying right now," East quickly dismissed him. "What's wrong wit' you?" he questioned Dos' thinking.

"What's wrong wit' me?" Dos snapped, gesturing with his hands toward the hospital. "Nigga, my father is laying shot up in the hospital is what the fuck is wrong with me."

"And you should be in there, praying he make it. Instead of out here talking reckless to me." East warned.

"Who is you to tell me what I should be doing? I ain't ask for your advice," he seethed.

"So, what's there to talk about then?" East replied becoming aggravated with the back and forth. He knew Dos was too hot tempered to ever think sensibly.

"You were always good at being the help," Dos asserted in a condescending tone. He eyed East up and down. "So, help."

"What the fuck you say?" East pressed him, so they were face to face.

Dos smirked. "You ain't deaf, nigga." He blew smoke from his mouth then tossed his cigarette to the ground. Neither of them was willing to back down. "My Pops been spoon feeding you. You should be out here in the daytime with a flashlight trying to find who did it. Unless you had something to do with it," Dos wondered aloud, eyeing East suspiciously.

"What would I get out of killing your Pops," East asked. "That would fuck up my money. I look stupid to you? Think about it," he said pointing to his head.

"I'm calling the shots for now. And I say, there's a green light on any and everybody. No exceptions." Dos made sure to emphasize his last statement so East knew that included him as well.

East chuckled. "Only because your father is in there right now," he said pointing towards the hospital. "And I know you ain't thinking straight. I'm gonna forget you just said that. We both know you don't want that smoke." East swallowed hard, maintaining his composure.

"Yeah?" Dos' jaw flexed.

"Yeah," East assured him. "You always wanted to be the boss right, Junior?" he called Dos by the name he knew he hated. "Here's your big chance," he countered then walked away.

"Tell me something East. Cause I can't seem to figure it out," Dos' words floated through the air stopping East in his tracks. "When did you turn into a jelly fish? Cause I can remember one time in particular, when you used to have that killer instinct. Remember? Pow!" Dos made a gun with his finger and pulled the trigger. He was referring to East murdering Tez.

East muscles flexed and twitched as he stormed back towards Dos. "What! You snake ass nigga, that was your fault." Without warning East punched Dos in the face rocking him backwards. "Fuck you," East shouted.

Dos pulled the gun from his waist and pointed it at East. Rio immediately jumped in grabbing the gun away from him.

"Yo, Dos. Chill. You can't do that out here. It too many people. You trippin'," Rio appealed to his good senses.

"That's the second time you pulled a gun on me," East nodded.

"Third times the charm," Dos seethed as he wiped blood from his mouth.

"You and I both know better than that but go handle your business, nigga. You the boss now, right? King of Miami," East said sarcastically clapping his hands. "If and when you decide you really wanna do something. You know where to find me." East shook his head then walked to his car. He decided that coming to the hospital today was a bad idea. He would check on Ricardo another time.

Rio approached Dos as East hopped in his car and drove off. He handed him back his gun. "All you gotta do is say the word."

"I know but fuck him." Dos was dismissive.

"He ain't really family, anyway," Rio said.

"Exactly," Dos agreed then headed back inside the hospital.

CHAPTER EIGHTEEN

East stood quietly in front of his mother's grave. His visit was long overdue. He had come to forgive and to ask for forgiveness. He brought flowers because he knew his mother would want and appreciate them. He didn't have much to say. He knew she had been watching him and she knew everything that had been going on in his life. They had always had that type of connection. He knew it was still there because he felt her every day. Even when he tried to ignore it. She was there. So instead of talking, he just sat there enjoying the peacefulness of being with his mother. Like he did the night she died. The flood of memories that came rushing back brought tears with it. He missed her so much. He was the man he was because of her and her sacrifices. Ebony had instilled all his morals and values. Everything that Samayah loved about him came from her. He sat there for hours without saying much.

Finally, he rose to his feet and dusted himself off. He kissed her headstone. "I love you, ma. And I promise it wouldn't take me this long to come back and see you."

East was startled from the sound of grass crunching under someone's feet. He looked away from his mother's headstone, expecting to see a groundskeeper. Instead, Lauryn was standing there. Although he could tell she was using sunglasses as a veil, probably to hide her red-rimmed eyes. Not a hair on her head was out of place. She wore a white tank top, skin-tight jeans, pink Christian Louboutin pumps and held a pink Chanel bag in one hand and a Starbucks cup in the other. *She was always put together*, he thought. Her way of distracting from the hurt she felt. That might have fooled everyone else, but East recognized the look. He had seen it before, during his younger days as her bodyguard.

"I didn't mean to interrupt," she said softly. "I wasn't even sure if it was you." East remained silent. She could see he was thrown off by her presence. "I'm here visiting my father. He's over there remember?" she pointed over her shoulder.

"That's right," East said, remembering as he looked in that direction.

"I'm sorry, I didn't speak the other day at the hospital."

"I understand," he assured her that he hadn't taken offense. "How is he?" he inquired about Ricardo's health.

Lauryn lowered her head, "Nothing has changed, yet." East nodded. "But it's nice seeing you again," she said. He had matured nicely since his days as one of her many bodyguards. He had always been her favorite.

"You too." East looked around as she stepped away. He noticed there was nobody shadowing her. "If you don't mind me asking, shouldn't there be someone with you?"

She stopped and turned to face him. "I gave them the day off," she revealed.

East smirked. He had always gotten the impression Lauryn hated having her every move being shadowed. With Ricardo in the hospital, she had taken the opportunity to move more freely. After a long pause, East said, "Well...be safe," and turned to walk away.

"Don't go," she blurted out suddenly, even

surprising herself. "If you don't mind. It would be nice to have you here. Sort of like old times." And for the first time a smile creased her face.

"I guess I can do that for an old friend," East said smiling back.

Lauryn was thankful he decided to stay and keep her company. Having East there wouldn't take away the pain, but it strangely gave her some comfort. When he stepped away to allow her privacy to grieve, she grabbed his hand to stop him, then pulled him closer for support. *He smells so good*, she thought to herself then let the thought go, turning her attention to her father. East kept her company until she finished her visit. When she was ready to leave, he escorted her to the parking lot. He opened her car door.

"Old habits die hard," she quipped.

East laughed. "Oh, you got jokes."

"I'm just kidding," she chuckled. "I can see that ain't your thing no more." She too recognized what everyone seen in East. He was a different breed. A charismatic street nigga that was a goon and a hustler, all in one. He was destined for greatness. He had too much potential not to.

"It's good to see you not dressed in black," he said seriously.

"You noticed," Lauryn appreciated that he had. She removed her shades and took him in completely. She studied his handsome face and her eyes zoomed in to the tattoos on his neck, she couldn't help but notice how he had aged into a sexy piece of eye candy. Although he was forbidden fruit, it didn't hurt to look.

"I always noticed," East returned the gesture. It was impossible not to. Lauryn did this thing with her eyes when she spoke. It was like a magnetic pull that drew people in. She had a captivating aura and could cast a spell with her alluring eyes.

"It feels good to be seen. You know...like a person and not some kind of trophy," she explained then laughed nervously as tears trailed down her face. She had so much bottled up emotions. She felt like she would explode.

"You've been through a lot," East said. "No one expects you to be superwoman, all the time."

"This is so embarrassing," she sighed and attempted to wipe her tears, only to be stopped by East."

"No apologies needed. If you need to cry...cry. It's like taking your soul to the laundromat."

"What you know about some Lyfe Jennings?" she asked, cracking a smirk through her tears.

"You'd be surprised what I know," East said.

"You'd be more surprised what you don't," Lauryn said. The tone of her voice suddenly changed.

"What don't I know? Tell me," East searched her eyes intensely. Despite Lauryn's calm exterior, there was now a different look in her eyes. The look of a woman who knew more than she was willing to say. It had appeared out of nowhere, almost involuntary. Her eyes seemed to hold secrets that were buried deep inside but dying to reveal themselves.

"There's always a few missing parts to everyone's story, East" she explained. Lauryn stared at him. For some reason, she felt comfortable. That wasn't always the case for her being around men that worked for her husband. Most never said a word to her and were afraid to even make eye contact. They made her feel like a thing and not a person. East was different. He didn't treat her like that. He made her feel real, like she did before she was the *boss' wife*. Secretly, Lauryn despised that title. It put her in a bubble. She wasn't allowed to be herself. But in East's presence, she felt freedom. Even if it was only for the brief moment that they stood alone in the parking lot of a cemetery. It was a feeling she hadn't experienced in a long time.

"What's that supposed to mean?" he pressed her about her statement.

"Nobody is who they seem, but everybody is exactly who they are," she said.

"You're talking in riddle. If nobody is who they seem, then who are you? The real you," His mouth asked the question but the serious look in his eyes said so much more to Lauryn. It said he wanted to know the deepest parts of her. Not just the beautiful surface. No man had ever looked at her the way he did. It was so mesmerizing that it momentarily took her breath away.

"I'm just regular ol' me," she said softly. She stepped closer. The smell of his cologne invaded her nostrils again. She inhaled deeply. She didn't want to move. She just wanted to be still and enjoy his energy. It was refreshing.

"Believe me Lauryn, there is nothing regular about you. Any man who thinks that is a fool," his boldness shocked her. But it spoke to her soul.

"East stop," she blushed. "You can't be looking at me like that. Or saying those type of things," she said.

"I'm just being honest and calling it how I see it," he stated

Before he could finish, she kissed him. Something in her kiss shot through his body. It was electric. He wanted to pull away, but he didn't. She couldn't either. Instead, she leaned in towards him and kept kissing him, more passionately.

Suddenly, she backed away, breathless. "This is wrong," she said. 'I'm so sorry," she cried.

"It's ok," he tried calming her down.

When he tried to reply she quickly cut him off. "No East, this is wrong. I was wrong. We can't do this. We shouldn't be doing this," she said getting into her car in a feverish haste. "You need to forget this ever happened." She slammed the door and pulled off.

East stood frozen for a moment. Unsure of what had just happened. He had gotten caught up in the moment. "Fuck," he scolded himself. Ricardo's wife had just made a move on him. He shouldn't have stayed with her. He saw she was vulnerable. He hadn't thought about the consequences of his actions until it was too late. That wasn't like him. A mistake like that could cost him his life and rightfully so, he thought to himself. He knew better. She knew better. She might have just signed his death certificate. He only hoped Lauryn stayed true to her word and forgot it ever happened.

* * *

Lauryn rushed into the house. Closing the door, she leaned her back against it and exhaled, trying to calm her raging heart. Kissing East had given her a feeling that wasn't easily forgotten. After taking a few seconds to gather her thoughts, she headed straight upstairs to shower. A little while later, she descended the stairs into the kitchen and searched the cabinets for the biggest wine glass she could find. When she located it, she poured herself a glass of wine and took a few sips. She sat the glass on the marble countertop and enjoyed her view. The floor to ceiling glass patio doors in the kitchen, made the room feel like it extended outdoors to where the ocean was her backyard. From her position, she had a perfect view across the water to South Beach. At night, the strip would come alive with people. The buildings would light up with vibrant colors. The lights reflecting off the water created an amazing optic she enjoyed. A noise disturbed her from the calm and peacefulness she had found within her thoughts. Before she could turn around, someone grabbed her from behind and placed their hand over her mouth. She was easily overpowered and felt paralyzed with fear.

"Do what I say, and you won't get hurt," the intruder barked out instructions. "You understand?" Lauryn nodded her head. "That's a good girl," he said, caressing her hair and the side of her face.

Lauryn felt sick to her stomach as the man's

hands began exploring her body. She could feel him becoming aroused as he pressed his body against hers. She felt like her heart would leap from her chest at any moment. His hand made its way down to her waist. He easily untied her silk robe, exposing her naked breast and lace panties. When the air hit the beads of water that remained from her shower, her Hersey kiss nipples became erect. The intruder rubbed her breasts then squeezed them aggressively. Lauryn struggled against his grip as he had his way with her. Her next breath got stuck in her throat, feeling his hand over her crotch area. He began rubbing her clit through her panties. It was all happening so fast. She wanted to scream but no one would hear her. She was alone with the intruder and at his mercy. He yanked at her panties, forcefully ripping them away, giving himself a clear path to her shaved pussy. Lauryn grunted in pain as he plunged his two fingers into her. To both of their surprise, Lauryn was wet, something she couldn't help. It seemed to turn him on more, make his breathing become heavier in her ear.

"You like that shit, don't you bitch?" he taunted as he worked his fingers in and out of her roughly. "You up in this big house by yourself. No one to guard you or help you."

Lauryn began to grunt and groan from the pain. She tried to speak but his hand wrapped around her neck, squeezing the air from her lungs and muffling her words. She felt like she was on the verge of blacking out as he squeezed tighter.

"Shut up bitch?" he demanded harshly in her ear while continuing to stroke her with his fingers. Finally, he removed his hand from her neck.

Lauryn felt like she had just emerged from the deepest waters. She took in a deep breath of air then in a loud whisper, she cried out, "Oh my God, that feels so good."

She spun around and when her lips met Dos' lips, they melted into each other. Their tongues dancing with each other. Dos stuck his fingers in her mouth allowing her to taste her own juices. Lauryn licked his fingers clean. They began tearing at each other's clothes, stripping down until they were both naked in the middle of the kitchen.

"Did you remember to turn off the cameras," she asked.

"Of course." Dos pressed her back against the kitchen's island then lifted her up on the counter. Lauryn spread her legs, resting them on his shoulders, grabbing the back of his head and guiding his face into her pulsating lotus flower. Dos worked his tongue like a helicopter propeller inside her pussy. Lauryn held on to anything she could grab, first the counter then his head, eventually his ears as he sucked and slurped on her swollen clit. Lauryn's moans grew louder. She had given all her security detail the day off for this reason. Her legs became weak and began to shake, and her muscles tensed up as Dos took her body to its own personal nirvana.

"Oh baby, right there. Yes," she cried out as her mouth fell open from the orgasm surging through her body.

Dos stroked himself as Lauryn sat up and slid off the counter. She turned around and bent over the counter. Using both her hands to spread her ass cheeks, she gave him ease access to her pink wetness. He eased his rock-hard manhood into her juicy pussy and quickly found his rhythm. Lauryn moved her hips taking all of him inside of her. Their bodies made loud noises as their flesh slapped together. Lauryn call his name while she climaxed over again. Dos gripped her ass and thrusted harder, digging deeper inside of her with every powerful stroke. He began to moan, feeling his climax building. She could feel him throbbing inside of her walls. She began to throw her ass back at him and in short, circular movements until she heard him let out a primal scream. Dos pulled out of her pussy, stroking himself until he spilled his seed on her round ass.

She fell forward. He laid on top of her back as she rested her body on the counter. Their chest heaving up and down, trying to catch their breaths. A few minutes passed before Lauryn moved, walking out the kitchen and up the stairs to the bedroom. Dos followed behind her and they picked up right where they left off.

CHAPTER NINETEEN

Early the next morning, a knock on the door woke Rio from his sleep on the couch. He had been too tired to make it to his bedroom the night before and crushed on his sofa. He stretched his arms towards the ceiling and rubbed his nose while yawning. He got up as the knocking continued and walked over to the door. Looking through peephole, he saw an old head junkie named Freddy, wearing a worn out Made in Dade t-shirt. He always came around to wash Rio's car for money or drugs.

"It's too early for this shit," Rio sighed and mumbled to himself. He was still half sleep. "Freddy, I should beat ya muthafuckin' ass, coming to my crib this early in the morning," he ranted as he snatched the door open. Rio stuttered his next words, caught by surprise. A dark-skinned gunman with huge jail muscles had Freddy by the back of his shirt with a big gun to the back of his head. The gunman forced his way inside the apartment, followed by another gunman that quickly stuck his gun in Rio's face.

"What the fuck is going on?" Rio uttered no longer asleep. He had been caught slipping, his gun was still sitting on the coffee table next to a duffle bag.

"Get the fuck on the floor, fuck nigga," the dark-skinned gunman told Rio as he slammed Freddy to the floor and put his foot on his back. The other gunman did the same to Rio. "Watch them niggas," the dark skinned one told his partner. "If they move pop they muthafuckin' ass, you hear me?" Then he began searching the apartment. He didn't have to search long. Rio had left money and two bricks of coke in the open duffle bag on the table. With all the goods already neatly stuffed inside the bag, the gunman walked back over to Rio and began brutally pistol whipped him, over and over. Rio's face became a bloody mess, so did his shirt. "I should kill you right now," he threatened with his gun to Rio's head. He pulled his phone from his pocket and dropped it on the floor next to Rio. "Call him," he barked.

"Call who?" Rio groaned.

"Don't play with me, nigga. You know who," the gunmen shouted. "Pick it up and call Dos, right now."

"I can't see," Rio whimpered. There was blood pouring into his eyes and his face continued to leak.

The gunman looked over to his partner that was standing over Freddy. He nodded and without hesitating the man, fired two shots into Freddy's head. The dark skin gunmen calmly squatted down next to Rio with his gun aimed at him and said, "Dial the fuckin' number." Struggling with his vision, Rio did his best to do just that.

* * *

Dos sat at the foot of the bed that Lauryn shared with his father, getting dressed. She lay there studying his every move. To her, Dos was everything Ricardo wasn't; young and aggressive. He just wasn't the boss yet. That was something they were both hoping to change in the very near future. Dos felt like a God. He saw the world as his and everything in it he should have, including his father's beautiful wife.

"What happened Dos? Why is he still alive?" Lauryn complained. "You promised to take care of it. Instead of burying him, I'm having to keep visiting him in the hospital and fake tears for them nosey ass nurses." Lauryn folded her arms across her chest frustrated and disappointed. "I don't know why you just didn't do it yourself."

Since Dos lacked the patience it took to wait his turn, he had tried to speed up the process. Things hadn't gone exactly as planned, Ricardo wasn't dead. Dos' excessive amount of ambition made him believe that any rule could be broken except for one.

"How many times do I have to tell you, I'm not about to shoot my own father," he quickly grew angry at the suggestion. "I'll get him killed but I'm not doing that," he insisted. Dos wanted Ricardo dead, but he didn't have the guts to do it himself.

Lauryn crawled up behind him like a temptress and wrapped her arms around him, and rested her head on his back. "If you did it, you'd know it would be done right," she insisted softly in his ear, trying her best to convince him to change his mind.

"What did I just say?" he barked, breaking free from her embrace and standing up. "I'll figure out another way. Don't worry about it," he reassured her, shaking his head as he admired her naked body. "How's it going with East?" he asked. "When this shit all goes down, we gotta make sure it looks like it was him." Dos ran his hand over his face.

"I'm working on it," she promised.

"Good. You keep doing your part and I'll do mine." Before he could continue, his phone rang, grabbing his attention away from Lauryn. He walked over to the nightstand and picked it up. "Yeah," he huffed.

"Dos—" Rio cried. The gunman snatched the phone away before he could finish. He placed it to his ear.

"Rio," Dos called out into the phone.

"This Dos?" a voice asked aggressively from the other end of the phone.

"Who this?"

"Is this Dos," the voice repeated.

"Yeah, who this?" Dos asked calmly.

"This Blue, nigga."

Dos eyes widened and his face looked like he saw a ghost.

"What's wrong?" Lauryn whispered with concern, seeing the worried look on his face.

Dos knew the name Blue well. He was Kev's older brother. He was a straight menace on the streets; an old school jack boy turned hustler, but he was also a killer. Up until recently had been locked up but he was home and out for vengeance. "What's up?" Dos challenged. "The fuck you on my line for?"

"You killed my brother," Blue accused.

"I don't know what the fuck you're talking about. And from the sound of it, neither do you," Dos claimed.

"Before he died, my little brother told me about a job he was supposed to do for you," Blue said. Dos thought his heart stopped when he heard that. "You one slimey ass nigga to hire somebody to off your Pops. No need to worry tho. When I catch up to you, I'm putting you, your faggot ass father and anybody else connected to you in a body bag. For free. Starting with your cousin right here," Blue declared.

Dos heard Rio scream through the phone, followed by gunshots. There was a brief moment of silence before the phone went dead. Dos was so angry he tossed his phone across the room.

"What just happened?" Lauryn shouted in a panic after seeing his reaction. She had heard the conversation and the gunshots.

Dos pinched the bridge of his nose then gave her a menacing look. "Nothing! I got it under control."

"Under control? Really?" she shouted before hushing her tone. "Your father's not dead and somebody besides us knows you we're behind it. Seems to me, all you did was make the shit worse. What if someone else finds out?" She knew the consequence if Ricardo somehow found out about her and Dos' betrayal. They would both be dead. The thought alone gave her the bubble guts. Ricardo was not a man of mercy. Whoever he deemed responsible would pay with their lives.

Lauryn stood up from the bed and grabbed her silk Versace robe to cover her naked body. She headed over towards the balcony door in her bedroom and pulled the drapes back slightly, giving her a view of the pool and allowing the sunlight to beam into the bedroom.

Dos marched over and spun her around forcefully. He gripped her face firmly, squeezing it with his hand. "Let me tell you something. Ain't nobody gonna find out shit, unless you open your fuckin' mouth," he said. His eyes were threatening. He let her face go, mushing it away. "I said I'll take care of it and I will." His overflowing confidence was on full display. "Get dressed and take your ass to the hospital. What kind of wife ain't by her husband's side around the clock after he's been shot, anyway? Focus on that. And focus on East," he seethed then walked out the room.

Lauryn sighed deeply, fear surging all through her body. She had no other choice but to trust in Dos. They weren't soulmates by any stretch of the imagination. They weren't even in love, although the sex between them was lovely. Dos took her body to unimaginable places and hit spots Ricardo couldn't reach anymore. They were just two souls with an axe to grind against a common enemy. Lauryn wanted to be free from Ricardo's control and Dos wanted to be king. As the saying goes; *The enemy of my enemy is my friend.*

CHAPTER TWENTY

The next night, Dos' phone rang as he drove around the city looking for Blue. He sighed deeply seeing Jasmine's name flashing across his screen. It was at least the tenth time she had called. He had too much going on to deal with her bullshit. He knew if he didn't answer she wouldn't stop calling anytime soon. He decided to answer it, in case it had something to do with his son. "Damn. What!" he shouted into the phone.

"You can't just ignore my calls, Dos. We have a son, in case you forgot," Jasmine said.

"Yeah. I can't forget that," he said sarcastically.

"Why would you ever want to?" she questioned.

"I never want to forget my son. Just wish I could

forget his annoying ass mother," he shot back. "What do you want? I got lot of shit going on right now."

"Yeah I heard. The streets is talking," she replied.

"That's your fuckin problem now," Dos snapped. "You always got an open ear for someone to say some shit about me. I told you before, you need to stop listening to them hoes at your job."

"Whatever, you just need to be safe. You got people out here that love and care about you," Jasmine confessed her feelings. The phone went silent for a moment, Dos refusing to respond to her last statement. After a long pause, Jasmine continued, "Anyway, I need money for Tre's day care."

"I'll bring it to you in a couple days. Shit is crazy right now."

"It can't wait til then," she whined. "I've been calling you and you haven't been answering. It has to be paid in the morning or they're gonna put him out of school," she complained. "If they put him out, I have to reapply just to get him on the list again. And then, ain't no telling how long it will be before he could go back. You remember how long it took him to get him in there the first time—"

"Yeah. Yeah. Okay." Dos sighed into the phone then cut her off. "Where you at now?"

"I'm at work," she said with an attitude, stating the

obvious. Jasmine knew Dos could hear the loud music bumping in the background.

"Aight. I'll be up there In a few on my way."

A short while later, Dos pulled up and parked a block away from the club. If Blue knew he was responsible for killing Kev, there was no telling who else knew. He had to be on point, not just from Blue but the police too. Dos got out and tucked his gun into his waist. He headed inside the club. Once inside, Dos bumped into a dude that bought bricks from him. He looked at Dos like he had saw a ghost.

"What the fuck you doing in here, my nigga?" the dude yelled over the music, dapping Dos.

"I'm lookin' for somebody," Dos said unwilling to give any more information than that. He didn't need everyone knowing that Jasmine was his baby mother and that she worked in the club.

"I heard about your cousin Rio. That shit fucked up," the dude said shaking his head. "I heard niggas looking for you too, for killing Kev."

"I'on know what the fuck you're talkin bout my nigga. You police?" Dos asked quickly putting an end to the conversation, moving past him and heading for the bar, where Jasmine was.

When Jasmine spotted Dos coming through the crowd of people, her insides began to bubble. She filled with nervous energy. She turned her head, making eye contact with Blue. He was posted in the cut, at the end of the bar with a hat pulled low over his face. He followed her eyes in Dos' direction.

When Dos approached the bar, he squeezed between two female waitresses waiting for their orders. He admired their bodies, looking them up and down and smiling. They smiled back, appreciating the fine-looking stranger in their midst.

"Hey daddy, you need some help?" one of them flirted with him.

"I'm good. But definitely some other time another place too," he said and smirked. "Jasmine!" he yelled over the music trying to get her attention.

She glanced over her shoulder at him from the other end of the bar. Her heart was pounding in her chest as she watched Blue get up from his seat and began to circle around to where Dos was standing.

Dos called out to Jasmine again, this time waving her to him. "I don't have all night, c'mon," he shouted, reaching in his pocket for the money she needed. She hesitated to move. He instantly picked up on her weird behavior. Something was off. He could tell by the look on her face. Her eyes looked away from him and when he followed them, he spotted what she was looking at.

Suddenly, gunfire erupted inside the club. Panic ensued within seconds, people scrambling in every direction. Dos ducked to the floor and pulled out his gun as the gunshots continued to fly his way. Blue was relentlessly firing. Dos searched through the crowd until he spotted Blue's exact position. He popped up from the floor and started returning fire.

It was raining bullets inside the club. Both men shooting at each other through the crowd of running people. Blue empty his clip. Disappointed and frustrated that he had missed his chance, he slipped out the back of the club. Blending in the chaos as Dos stood in the middle of the club, in the mix of people shooting.

Finally, Dos slipped into the crowd, hitting the front door with everyone else. He headed straight for the car. When he got outside, police were coming down the streets. He jumped into his Benz and sped away.

Dos phone rang as he was driving. He was already planning how he was going to move on Blue, when he saw Rio's name come across the scene. That meant it could only be one person.

"Bitch ass nigga, you missed. You're a dead man," Dos barked in the phone. His voice was filled with emotion and adrenaline.

"Fuck you. Suck my dick. You're living on borrowed time," Blue laughed and banged on him.

Dos gritted his teeth as the phone call ended. "I'ma kill that nigga!" he shouted, banging his fist on the steering wheel. Jasmine's face appeared in his mind. He noticed how she was acting funny back at the club and how she hadn't called to check on him. "Foul ass bitch. I'ma kill her too," he seethed. His phone began ringing again. This time it was Lauryn. He ignored the call, but she called right back, then again and again. Finally, he answered. "What's up? What you want?" his adrenaline mixing with anger as he spoke.

"What's up son. It's good to hear your voice."

Dos' heart skipped a beat, hearing his father's voice on the phone. "Hey...Hey Pops." Dos voice was unsteady from shock and surprise. "When you wake up," he asked.

"Not how you feeling or good to hear your voice? Just when did you wake up?" Ricardo questioned with a horse laugh.

"You know what I meant, Pops," Dos calmed his nervousness. "Something crazy just happened. I ain't thinking straight, right now."

"Come up to the hospital in the morning and you can tell me all about it. For now, I'm gonna get some more rest. I just wanted to hear your voice." Ricardo said.

"You do that," Dos said. "Oh and Pops,"

"What," Ricardo replied.

"I love you. It's good to have you back from the dead."

"It's good to be back," Ricardo said. "By the way, Lauryn is gonna take you to meet somebody tomorrow night. I need you to go on my behalf."

"Ok. No problem Pops. Whatever you need."

"Good, good. I'll talk to you later," Ricardo said then hung up.

Dos let the phone linger next to his ear for a second, then let it fall to the seat.

* * *

Dos sat in his car in front of Jasmine's apartment building with his gun on his lap. He had been downstairs for over an hour, contemplating killing her. Every time he convinced himself to get out the car and do it, his son's face would flash before his eyes. He was so conflicted. He had never been so sure and unsure of anything before in his life. Jasmine's betrayal should be dealt with one way, death. She had earned it, but had he pushed her to that point? He questioned himself. And if he was being truthful with himself, the answer would be yes. He knew it. She had never done anything but tried to love him. He in return gave her his ass to kiss. He had turned a good girl bad and it had almost cost him his life. But should it cost her hers was the question. Jasmine deserved to die. But his son, Tre, didn't deserve to grow up without a mother like he had. When it boiled down to it, Dos loved his son more than he hated his baby's mother.

He took the clip out the gun and tossed it on the passenger seat. He didn't trust himself. He got out the car and walked inside Jasmine's building. He put his key in the front door of her apartment and walked in.

Jasmine was sitting in the living room, holding their son in her arms. It was like she was waiting for him. Her heart felt like it leaped into her throat when Dos walked into the house. He had a crazed look in his eyes. Tre called out for his *Da-Da*, as soon as he spotted Dos but he ignored him. Tears began falling from Jasmine's eyes, noticing the black latex gloves on his hands. She knew what he was capable of. She wasn't naïve to the type of man he was.

Dos walked over and sat down next to her. He knew being so close to her made her uncomfortable. He took his son out her arms and sat him on his lap and began playing with him. Never once did he make eye contact with Jasmine. Finally, he spoke but when he did, his voice was eerily calm. "I know what you did."

Jasmine started to cry harder. "I'm sorry, Dos."

"No, you're not," he replied.

"I swear," Jasmine pleaded. "He threatened to kill me and Tre, if—"

Dos stopped the words from coming out her mouth by wrapping his hand around her throat. "Don't use my son as an excuse, bitch," he gritted his teeth as he squeezed. "I should kill you right now," he growled as spit flew from his mouth. "I want you to take Tre and move back to New York. You got 48 hours to leave. You understand me? If I ever see your fucking face again, I'm gonna kill you. I promise. When I wanna see my son, I'll send for him." Dos released his grip on her neck. Jasmine began choking, coughing and gasping for air. Dos kissed his son on the cheek then sat him next to her. He rose to his feet and tossed a stack of hundreds on the coffee table then looked back at her. She had tears racing down her face and snot coming out of her nose. She sat deathly still. She was once so beautiful to him, know all he saw was a woman who tried to set him up. She was disgusting. "When I come back through here in two days, I'm not leaving my gun in the car. So, you better be gone," he said then walked out the house, not bothering to close the door behind him.

CHAPTER TWENTY-ONE

Lauryn sat by the window in the hospital, watching her husband sleep. She felt like her world was falling apart in front of her eyes. It made her sadder than it did angry, still tears filled her eyes as she thought about it. She had been under Ricardo's thumb long enough. She needed out. She felt like his hostage. He monitored her every waking moment. Her bodyguards were not there for protection but more to keep her captive. They reported everything back to Ricardo. There were cameras all through her home. Ricardo said they were for their safety. She knew he used them to keep an eye on her when he wasn't around. He had only trusted her to be alone with Dos and before that East. That was how her and Dos eventually became intimate. Spending time together, they realized they shared a similar hatred for Ricardo. They hatched a plan that benefitted the both of them but now it was falling apart quickly. Ricardo would be coming home any day now, which meant back to her dreaded routine life. She enjoyed him being in the hospital honestly. It gave her a bit of freedom. She sent the guards away on days and enjoyed just being a normal person. That was surely over now. Tears danced down her face as she recalled how she had gotten to this place in her life.

The fifty foot, state of the art yacht smoothly cruised the waters of the Florida Keys, somewhere between the Atlantic Ocean and the Gulf of Mexico. Old man Al had a glass of cognac in one hand and a cigar in the other as he relaxed in a chair on the deck, enjoying the view. This was his second yacht and he spared no expense this time around. It was lavishly decorated with Gold faucets and sinks, mink rugs and state of the art entertainment.

"What do you think, beautiful ain't it?" he asked the man sitting across from him.

"Yes, it is," Ricardo said. He wasn't talking about the boat or the water. His eyes were locked on Old Man Al's 20 year old daughter, as she navigated the boat through the sea. She was gorgeous. More beautiful than any woman

Ricardo had seen before. Her skin looked like it had been kissed by the sun and her eyes looked like he could see heaven in them.

"How bout I let you use my boat, anytime you want, until I'm able to pay you back the money," Al said.

Ricardo leaned back in his chair and looked out at the water. "I'm not really into boats, Al."

"This is not any ol' boat," Al explained. "I paid top dollar for this yacht. This is top shelf shit you cruising on," he bragged and laughed.

"That's the thing. I'm trying to get paid in dollars too. I loaned you cash. I want cash in return," Ricardo commanded. "You said you were in debt to the cartel. I tried to help you. You fucked me. I've been more patient with you than most, out of respect, but I can't guarantee you how much longer that's gonna last. And know you got the nerve to ask me for more."

"I know. I know. I appreciate you. I just need a little more cash, Rico," By calling Ricardo by his childhood nickname, Al was banking on the history between the two of them. Before Ricardo was a street dude on the come up with dreams of being a boss, he was a boxer and before that, he was a local kid with a dream of becoming world champ one day. That's where Old Man Al knew him from. Al was the biggest drug dealer in Miami at that time. He used to look out for Ricardo big time. Keeping money in his pocket,

giving him cars to drive, even getting him his first piece of pussy. Anything to keep him out of trouble, out the streets and on the right path. When his boxing career didn't turn out like everyone thought, Ricardo turned to Al then too. And like always Old Man Al took care of him. He put Ricardo in the game and before he knew it, he was living larger than he ever had as a boxer. After his first taste of street money, there was no turning back for Ricardo. He jumped into the streets head first. Now he had outgrown his teacher, like a fish that outgrew the pond.

"I put you in the game baby. You owe me," Al said.

"I don't owe you shit. Whatever I owed you, I done repaid twice over," Ricardo reminded him.

"Just give me the money and hold on to my boat until I can pay you back," Al pleaded.

"I told you, this ain't my thing. I wouldn't know the first thing to do with it," Ricardo said.

"You sail this muthafucka! C'mon Rico, it gotta be something we can work out?"

Ricardo grew quiet then his eyes turned towards Al's daughter Lauryn again. He wanted her more than he wanted the money he was owed. "I think I got a way we can clear your tab and I can help you out," Ricardo smiled.

"What's that?" Al asked with a smile.

"What if you gave me your daughter's hand in marriage and I gave you the money you needed," Ricardo

sat back in his seat and waited for an answer.

"Lauryn?" Al laughed thinking Ricardo had to be joking. But when he found himself the only one laughing, he became serious as well. "My daughter is only 20. She's a little girl," he said angrily.

"I don't mean you no disrespect Al but she ain't no little girl. She all woman," Ricardo explained.

"In looks only but not in the mind. Not for a man like you," Al replied

"C'mon Al, it's not like I'm trying to make her part of my Harem or anything. I'm taking bout marriage. My last name. A lifetime commitment. I'm just asking for your blessing. You've raised her and gave her nothing but the best. I can continue to do that. You know me and what I'm about. You know she will be well taken care of. The cartel has cut you off. You're drowning in debts. Even if I gave you the money, how long you think your lifestyle gonna last?" he questioned giving the old man something to think about.

As they pulled the boat back into the harbor, Ricardo approached Lauryn and winked at her. She smiled, and he returned the gesture. "How are you doing, I'm Ricardo," he introduced himself.

"I know who you are," she smiled. "I'm Lauryn."

"I already know," he told her. "You're a very beautiful woman," he complimented causing her to blush. She was *flattered by the attention. She had been raised by a hustler and she knew a boss when she saw one. Ricardo was definitely that. "Your future bright, baby. From now on you gonna be mine."*

Lauryn giggled. She thought he was joking but he wasn't.

"I'm serious. You gonna be my wife," Ricardo explained to her.

"Huh?" she was confused.

"Do you love your father?" he smoothly asked.

"Of course."

"So, you would do anything for him, right?" Ricardo questioned.

"Yes," she replied once again.

"Your father owes some very important people a lot of money, baby girl. A whole lotta of money. He can't afford to pay. In our line of business, that's not good for business. I've killed men for far less," he said with such seriousness that Lauryn felt it in her chest. "I respect your father to the upmost. I don't want to see nothing happen to him. So, I'm willing to help. We worked out a deal. A way for him to pay off his debt. Ain't that right Al?" Ricardo put his hand on Al's shoulder.

"Daddy," Lauryn called out to him confused.

"I don't want to force you. I'm not into that. I'm not trying to be your pimp or nothing like that. I want you to

be my wife." Ricardo declared. *"But I must tell you that if you deny my request and your father can't pay those people he owes. They will kill him,"*

Tears were now building in the wells of Lauryn's eyes. She knew about her father's gambling problem and drug problems. She watched as all their possessions slowly disappeared over the years, but this was the lowest of the lows. This was rock bottom.

"Daddy?" she cried out to him again her eyes pleading with fear.

Al looked deflated and defeated. He was so ashamed he couldn't even look his daughter in the eye. "I don't have anything else baby. Their gonna kill me," he pleaded. "But look, baby girl, you don't have to do anything you don't want to." The strings of his heart were being pulled from every which way. He saw the fright and confusion in Lauryn's eyes. But what crushed him even more was he knew she would do anything to spare him. Loves sacrifice.

"I'm gonna treat you like a queen. You won't want for nothing," Ricardo told her. "But I need an answer, right now. Time is money and your father can't afford to waste another second. Their gonna kill him," he emphasized

"Ok, Ok!" she said. It was almost as if the word slipped out involuntarily, there was no thought, no apprehension. It was life and death. Her father's life or death. The choice was easy.

"Thank you, baby," Al sighed in relief.

"You're the real winner in the family, baby," Ricardo said sarcastically to Lauryn. "You gained a husband and didn't lose your father. Sounds like good math to me," he shrugged.

Lauryn was silent, and her body was stiff. The back of her throat became dry and she tried her hardest to swallow the knot that formed in it. She couldn't believe or understand why this was happening to her. Why this man just came and changed the whole course of her life and destroyed her father's existence for what she knew it to be. Lauryn, looked towards her Dad and decided against calling out for him again, he was defeated, and she felt it, she could feel his weakness and failure oozing from his pores. She let out a tear and decided she will now be his strength.

"I'll have Tez drop the money off later, OG," Ricardo said. "Don't fuck it up. Cuz ain't no more where that came from," he advised.

Old Man Al didn't heed the advice. He took the money Ricardo gave him and instead of paying off his debt. He tried doubling it by betting on some horses. He lost. And a few days later, Al relaxed on the deck of the yacht enjoying the sunset. When he finished the drink in his glass, he placed it down in front of him. He picked up the gun on his side as tears began to cloud his vision. He thought by handing over his daughter, he had saved his own life. But the shame he felt was eating him alive and made him not want to go on living. His gambling addiction had made him a poor excuse for a man and an even worse father. Lauryn was truly better off without him. His only joy was knowing she would be taking care of in a way he could no longer provide for her. After all, he had groomed Ricardo himself. He just wouldn't make the wedding.

Suddenly, the sound of a single gunshot pierced the air, disturbing the calm and peacefulness, causing a flock of seagulls to fly away. The chirping of birds overhead were immediately followed by the thud of the gun falling from Al's dead hand.

Lauryn wiped the tears running down her cheeks as she thought about her father. He would have moved Heaven and Earth for her. All these years later, the pain remained. Ricardo kept his word. He married her and she wanted for nothing. He had given her the best that life had to offer. But he treated her like a possession and not his wife. She felt like a prisoner. She was convinced Ricardo would never see her as anything more than a payoff for a debt. She was his beautiful trophy. She was there to be seen and not heard. Lauryn wasn't an evil woman, she just wanted out and knew he would never let her be free. Watching him sleep the thought of killing him, crossed her mind. She walked over to the bed and stood over him. It would be so easy to put a pillow over his face and rid herself of him. She reached for the pillow at the foot of the bed. At first her hands trembled but soon they steadied as she contemplated murder. Then she heard the door to the room open and looked up to see the night nurse entering. She placed the pillow down on the bed and smiled, stepping aside to allow the nurse to check on Ricardo. Lauryn had tears in her eyes and stepped out the room for some air.

CHAPTER TWENTY-TWO

Flaco cruised through the streets in his old neighborhood in Opa-Locka. He pulled up in front of the corner store and parked. It was nice and sunny outside. The type of day that reminded him why he loved being from Miami so much. The weather, the women and the weed.

"You want something out of here?" he asked his baby mother who sat in the passenger seat and his daughter in the backseat.

"No, just hurry up, so we can take her to the beach. She's excited," she said looking back at their daughter in the backseat

Flaco smiled when he looked at his beautiful

daughter, "Ok, I'll be right back," he said then got out the car and entered the store. When he entered, he was greeted by the cute, young Spanish female behind the counter. "Hey, Flaco. Long time no see," she said.

"What's up lil' mami, where's your old man?" he asked of the old guy that had owned the store since he was a kid.

"He's off today," she replied.

"Let me get two Swishers," he said then headed for the back of the store to grab a Sprite to mix with his lean. His drink of choice.

As he walked down the aisle, a man entered the store behind him. Flaco never paid him any attention. The promethazine and codeine in his system had him floating. His street senses weren't as sharp as they should've been. His mind was on having fun with his girl and daughter at the beach. He opened the door of the freezer to grab a soda when he felt a gun pressed into his lower back.

"What's good lil' nigga? You trying to live or die today? Turn around."

Flaco released the soda and did as he was told. When he turned around, his eyes grew wide. Dos was aiming a gun at his stomach, just out the view of the girl in front at the counter. "Yo what's good homie?

What's this about?" Flaco asked. He could tell by Dos' line of questions, that he was there to negotiate.

Dos checked him for a gun but found none. "Damn, you really out here slippin'," he laughed. "Look outside," he instructed. When Flaco turned to look, there were two dudes standing near his parked car. "Your daughter in that car, right?" Dos asked rhetorically.

Flaco lowered his head in defeat. He didn't have to answer for Dos to know. "Just tell your people to chill," he said calmly like he was rattled but they both knew better. The beads of sweat forming on his forehead told a different story. His heart was pounding in his chest. He didn't know why Dos was coming at him like he was.

"Calm down. If I wanted to kill you, you'd be dead already. I just want to talk," Dos said with a condescending smile

"Why you ain't just say that then? Instead of all this," Flaco asked.

"Cuz, I wanted to make sure I had your undivided attention," Dos said sarcastically as he lowered the gun.

"Well if you got something to say, say it," Flaco sounded annoyed and uninterested.

"I'm willing to look out for you, if you willing to

look out for me," Dos offered.

"What you talkin'" Flaco inquired.

"East," Dos said bluntly.

"Nah. No. Nah," Flaco shook his head quickly. Dismissing the idea altogether.

"Think about it first, before you turn me down," Dos said calmly, his eyes glancing back outside of the store. Flaco followed his eyes with his own. "This is an opportunity of a lifetime," Dos said.

"Yeah, so why you offering it to me?' Flaco wondered aloud, shifting in his stance.

"Why not?" Dos replied. "I know deep down inside you can't be happy with the way things are in Liberty City. I heard you running one of the spots by yourself now but still," Dos let his words linger.

"I'm good where I'm at. I'm doing just fine," Flaco chest swelled with pride.

"C'mon, how long you gonna tell that lie to yourself, lil' homie? Dos asked. "You the fourth man in a three man group. You're getting crumbs off the next nigga table," Dos moved closer to him, now they were both looking out at the car. "Your daughter shouldn't be eating crumbs bro. I know you know that. I know you wanna take care of her properly. Get her and her mother out them shitty ass projects. Get her a little dog, a backyard with a fence," Dos nodded.

"I know. I got a seed too. There's nothing I wouldn't do for him," he said appealing to the fatherhood in Flaco. "You can't do that being East's errands boy. You ain't come up with them, it's obvious." Dos looked him up and down judging his appearance. "Where is your new ride? Your new crib? East, Screw and Que only gonna look out for East, Screw and Que. Who looking out for you?"

"I'm listening," Flaco said.

Dos could see the light come on in Flaco's eyes. "Yeah, I thought you would. I can put you in position, so you'll never need them niggas again. Things about to change in the city. When it does, you wanna make sure you're playing for the winning side."

"So, what I got to do?" Flaco asked.

"It's simple. Put my number in your phone and answer when I call."

"That's it?" Flaco asked surprised and a bit suspicious.

"That's it." Dos smiled.

* * *

The mild summer air flowed with ease through East's living room window. He sat next to Screw, rolling up some weed. "I needed to talk to you, bro," East said sparking the weed and taking a pull. "You know we go back to the sandbox. And we were always like family," he choked out his words along with the weed smoke. He passed the weed to Screw and continued, "I'm just gonna come out with the shit. Me and Samayah been dating for like a year. You were locked up and we didn't know how to tell you. And when you came home, we just...." East let his words trail off. "We ain't told Ms. Ang either. I know that don't make it no better."

Screw inhaled the weed and blew smoke into the air. He remained quiet and emotionless. East couldn't get a read on him. Screw looked like a mad man tonight with his long, hair out and wild. His protection beads hanging around his neck.

"Say something, nigga," East said as he stared at him.

Screw just kept smoking, never passing the weed back to East. Finally, he looked over at him. "What you wanted me to say, my nigga? You looking for a blessing or something? I know it can't be that," he said sitting up and resting his arm on his knees. "Y'all been fucking around for a whole year already," Screw exhaled more smoke. "Y'all fucking around or y'all fucking around?" he asked seriously.

"Nigga, what the fuck does that mean?" East laughed.

"I mean you fucking with my sister for the right

now, or you fucking with her?" Screw inquired.

"I'm fucking with her. I love her," East proclaimed with no hesitation or bend in his words.

Screw got quiet again. He stared at East for what felt like forever. Like he was processing it all. "Look, if you tell me you love her. I believe you. You ain't never lied to me one time. So, I know if you say it you mean it. Shit, she been in love wit' yo ass since we was kids," he laughed. "I'm cool with it. Just give me some time to get used to it," he said and dapped East. He held on to his hand, "But real shit, y'all gotta tell moms."

East nodded in agreement then his phone rang interrupting them. He looked at the screen, it was a number he hadn't seen in a long time. He frowned his brow, wondering why Jasmine was calling him. He started not to answer but his curiosity got the better of him. "Hello," he said and was immediately bombarded with tearful cries and words. "Calm down. What? You're where?" East said. Jasmine was so distraught on the other end of the phone he could barely understand her. "Slow down. Slow down. You said what now?" as he got up from the couch and walked into the bedroom.

Jasmine proceeded to tell him everything that happened the other night at the club between Dos and Blue. East had already heard about it on the streets but he played dumb, allowing her to fill in all the blanks for him. Jasmine was more than happy to. She was pissed about being exiled to New York by Dos. Honestly, East thought she was lucky that was all she got but he never mentioned it. He just listened and when she was finished, he wished her the best and hung up. He walked back to the couch and sat down, lit up some weed as he digested all that Jasmine had told him. He had an idea.

CHAPTER TWENTY-THREE

Dos leaned against a black Rolls Royce Wraith and lit a cigar as he waited on the landing strip of Opa-Locka Executive airport. He liked listening to the sound of the private jets taking off into the night's sky. He was on edge, but the mixture of cigar smoke and the sound of the engines allowed a calming feeling to wash over him. He always had a fondness for aviation, something he inherited from his father, who taught him how to fly a plane when he was still a teenager. Dos removed the cigar from his mouth, exhaling a cloud of smoke, allowing it to dance in the night air. He watched a jet land at the opposite end of the strip. It began taxiing slowly as it approached him and pulled into a hangar that read Fontainebleau Aviation. It circled before stopping. When the engine came to a rest, the door let down. Dos smiled and rubbed his hands together. He grabbed two oversized bags off the ground then climbed the steps to board the jet. Two menacing looking bodyguards met him at the top, blocking his path. One took the bags out his hands. The other made Dos raise his arms and began frisking him. When he was done, he stepped aside ushering Dos into the cabin.

As he stepped inside, Dos found Jose Navarro seated, enjoying a plate of seared beef tenderloin and shrimp. A beautiful blonde stewardess stood next to him, refilling his glass of wine then made her way to the back of the luxurious cabin. Dos admired the interior of the private jet. It was the most extravagant he had seen. Navarro looked different than Dos imagined. He looked like an account not a vicious liaison for a Mexican drug cartel. He moved more cocaine than all the other cartels combined. There he was, *a legend in the flesh*, Dos thought. Although Ricardo had been in business with Navarro and the cartel for many years, this was Dos' first encounter with him. Dos didn't fully trust him. There was no loyalty or love with Navarro, only business. Once you were in bed with the cartel, it was hard to get out. Their partnerships usually ended in death.

"No smoking on my plane," Navarro informed Dos without making eye contact with him. When Dos removed the cigar from his mouth, the stewardess quickly approached, holding a glass of water for him to dump it in to. The cigar made a sizzling sound as it dropped into the water and fizzed out. "Have a seat," Navarro instructed, pointing to the empty chair in front of him. Once Dos sat down, he continued, "I was expecting your father. I thought he was doing much better. Is everything okay with my good friend?"

"He's still recovering," Dos informed him. But he is feeling much better. I promise you," Dos said while accepting the glass of Cognac from the lovely stewardess.

"I see," Navarro nodded. Usually Ricardo came alone. There was a time when Tez would accompany him. This was the first time Dos had come. For as long as they had been in business, that routine had always remained the same, until now.

"Our organization is going through a bit of a...transition," Dos explained. "My father wants to move in a different direction. Take a step back from the day to day operations. So, from now on, I'll be taking over," he said confidently.

"Says who?" Navarro said flatly with a laugh.

Dos had a quick temper, but he knew better than to show his anger in this instance. He was sitting across from one of the most powerful men in the world. It served him better to choose his next words wisely. "Just thought it was a natural succession."

"This is not some trust fund or birth right that is passed down, easily," he explained. "My trust and respect has to be earned. That can take a long time. I have to admit, I'm not comfortable with this sudden change in plans." He looked Dos up and down. "I like dealing with your father better. We've done business for quite a few years. In that time, he's never been arrested, never been short or done any bad business. A man like me, values things like that a lot," he said. Navarro stuck his fork into a piece of meat, inhaled it into his mouth and began chewing. The way he chewed with his mouth open, disgusted Dos but he wouldn't dare say a thing.

"You can inherit your father's power on the street but not necessarily his wisdom. Those are very big shoes to fill, my friend. You think you're capable of that?" The air inside the jet grew thick with tension as he awaited an answer.

Dos felt uncomfortable, but he didn't show it. It was too late to be weary now. "I wear my own shoes," he replied, full of machismo then sipped his drink. His phone rang but he pressed ignore.

"I like that," Navarro chuckled. He snapped his fingers and one of his men approached, handing Dos a heavy duffel bag. He looked Dos square in the eyes. "That's 25 kilos. As long as things don't change with my money, I don't see us having any problems moving forward," he instructed.

"It won't," Dos nodded, knowing that he didn't have any other choice but for it not to. There was no wiggle room with a man like Navarro. He could send a death squad with just a head nod. The two men shook hands and the deal was sealed.

Dos got off the jet and watched as it pulled out of the hangar before taking off. He never felt such power as he did at that moment. Now all he had to do was clean his plate. Blue was first on his list. He looked at his watch, that was being taking care of real soon. East was next then his father. Fuck killing two birds with one stone, Dos was trying to kill ants with a sledgehammer.

* * *

Blue's Barber Shop sat in the middle of the block. Dos had been there plenty of times to see Kev, so it was nothing to seed a crew through there. He had a two-man team sitting on the spot for over two weeks trying to get eyes on Blue. It was in the wee hours of the night when they finally spotted him and placed the call. Dos' crew of killer swarmed the block. They soaked the outside of the shop, including the front door and back door with gasoline. Blue had originally chosen the spot because of the location. That decision was about to cost him heavily. The Molotov Cocktails came crashing through the windows, setting the shop ablaze. Just as expected, Blue and his men began scrambling inside to save money and drugs. It was only after they saw the large blaze at the front and back entrances that they realized they were trapped. By then, it was too late, Dos' team of hitters were spraying the shop, gunning down anyone lucky enough to escape the fire.

By the time the fire trucks and police got to the scene there was nothing left to save. Just dead bodies burnt alive and thick black smoke. The smell of death permeated through the block. The stench of cooked cocaine was so thick in the air, neighbors felt high from breathing it in. Police had to wait a full two days for the smoldering ash to cool down, before they could begin their investigation of the scene. They still needed to wear mask when they were finally able to enter. Nobody knew but one person had managed to escape.

CHAPTER TWENTY-FOUR

East sat inside his apartment talking to Screw and Que. They were talking about the fire that had happened at Blue's barber shop days earlier. When Que, dropped a crazy revelation.

"I know a chick that lives next door to a bitch that was fucking the nigga Blue. She told me the nigga still alive," Que announced.

"Ain't no fucking way," Screw said.

"I'm telling you. She said he hopped her fence the night of the fire and limped into shawty back door," Que assured them.

"Go get the nigga," East declared.

"Why? That shit ain't got nothing to do with us,"

Screw dismissed.

"Trust me, I got a plan," he said remembering his conversation with a distraught Jasmine the night she was exiled. "It'll all make sense. Y'all go get the nigga."

"Aight, I'm gonna call Flaco, We'll go handle it." Screw said jumping up, excited to put in some gun work if need be.

"Nah, just y'all two," East explained. "I need Flaco to stay at the spot in the Rockies. I got to pick some bread up from him later. I need him to stay in that spot.," he said. "Que I need you to hit that chick you know and make sure she saw what she said she saw."

"I got you," Que said. The fly, young nigga knew all the hoes. It wouldn't be nothing to get the info. They dapped up and Screw and Que headed out.

On the drive Que got all the info. He found out that Blue was indeed held up in a small house on Kasim Street. Que sat in the passenger's seat while Screw drove the old, '98 Honda Accord. When they pulled onto Kasim Street, Screw got out, guns in hand. Que jumped behind the wheel, parked down the block and turned off the headlights. Screw hid behind some tall bushes on the side of the house with a direct view of the driveway. They waited and waited for what felt like hours. Finally, a grey Charger with black rims pulled into the driveway and turned off the engine. A thick, female in a skin-tight, short dress got out. The dress rose as she walked, exposing her panties. She didn't even bother to pull it down.

"No, I want to know why so many bitches calling your phone?" she barked, moving her head and hands back and forth.

"Bitch shut up. They think I'm dead. You ain't got nothing to worry about," Blue's voice boomed as he struggled to get out of the passenger side. He was trying to be lowkey, dressed in a hood with shades.

Screw knew he'd caught him slipping. He was too distracted arguing with the female to notice him creeping up. Screw snuck up behind them just as they made it to the front door. He didn't hesitate. He shot the female in the back of the head, knocking her lace front completely off her head. The force of the bullet made her crash into a wobbly Blue, knocking them both to the ground.

Blue never had the chance to go for his weapon, all he could do was cover his face as Screw pointed the gun at his head. Que raced down the block and skidded to a stop in front of the house.

"You coming with me." Screw demanded as he grabbed Blue.

"I ain't going nowhere," Blue challenged,

gangster to the end, trying to struggle against Screw.

BOOM!

Blue screamed in pain, reaching for his leg that was leaking blood from the gunshot. Screw wasn't one for games. He lifted Blue off the ground and Que helped stuff him in the trunk of the car. They slammed the trunk closed and peeled off.

* * *

"Yo, we got the nigga," Screw informed over the phone.

"I'll meet y'all at the spot in a few. I'm over here waiting on this nigga Flaco, right now," East said.

"Bet," Screw replied than hung up.

East looked down at his watch and he had to control his frustration. It was almost midnight and he was tired of waiting. "What the fuck is taking this nigga so long?" he sighed while lowering the music. East clenched his jaw and scanned the block. He was alone in his car, across the street from the Pork & Beans projects, the place he had grown up. His Glock .40 was resting on his lap. Shit was real in Liberty City and East wasn't trying to get caught slipping.

Inside the apartment, Flaco held a double Styrofoam cup in his hand as he paced the floor. Dos had promised him the world and everything in it damn near, if he took care of East. Tonight, was the night. He was sweating, nervously. This was his opportunity to step up. Move East out the way and become the man. Dos promised to take care of Screw for him as well. All he had to do was kill East and everything would go smooth. He thought about his beautiful daughter's face. He saw her smiling at him. That was all the fuel he needed. He gulped the last bit of lean from the cup grabbed the black bag containing the count and walked out the door.

Above the rustling trees, thick grey clouds hung over the city as an occasional streak of lightning flashed in the night sky. Although it was almost midnight, the stifling humidity hadn't diminished nor faded. The air was thick, hot and still. The steady hum of air conditioners echoed throughout the projects, mixing with Flaco's footsteps. Everything was right. It was a perfect night for murder. He spotted East parked across the street and walked towards him.

East spotted Flaco strolling towards him like he didn't have a care in the world, carrying a black bag full of money. What had once been a fresh, white wife beater covering the young man's slender, tattooed body. His long, thick dreads bounced with every leisure step he took. It was like he was moving in slow motion.

East lowered the window of his old school Chevy, letting the pungent smell of weed escape into the night air. "Damn my nigga, you're acting like I got all night," he said as they slapped five. "You know I hate that shit," he explained, taking the bag from the man's outstretched hand.

"My bad homie," Flaco answered.

"I gotta count this shit or is it all there?" East asked.

"Everything is right."

East noticed Flaco's lax demeanor and avoidance of direct eye contact. His lethargic speech and body language made it clear that he was high on more than just weed. "You gotta lay off the lean. That shit got you off point. You can't be moving like a snail out here. Especially when you carry my money," East advised.

So many thoughts were racing though the Flaco's mind that he couldn't form the words to reply. He no longer saw a friend when he looked at East. He saw opportunity. The chance to move up a few rungs on the street ladder and take better care of his daughter. At least that's what Dos had promised to him. East was in the way of all that.

When East turned away to sit the bag on the passenger seat, the timing was perfect. Flaco stepped closer to the car and in one motion pulled out his gun, pressing it to the back of East's skull. There was one last message to deliver before he sent a bullet through his brain.

"Dos said, it ain't nothing personal. You just in his way," then he squeezed the trigger.

Nothing happened. Just a loud hollow click but no bang. *Oh shit*, Flaco thought to himself as he squeezed again with the same result. *The shit jammed.* The realization seemed to make time stand still. His heart sank into his stomach and his eyes grew wide, filling with confusion and shock. The mixture of codeine and promethazine in his system made him slow to react. Had he been sharp and sober, he might have stood a chance. He lowered the gun trying to re-cock it.

It was too late now, East reacted swift and precise. Turning, lifting the gun from his lap and squeezing off rounds. Gunfire lit up the street, barking like a vicious Pitbull. Each bullet slamming into Flaco's chest like a Mack truck on fire. He staggered backwards, reaching for his chest. His dingy white t-shirt turning crimson as life begin to leak from his body. He fell face up on the ground. Death would be all he got for his betrayal. East opened the car door and got out. His sneakers hitting the ground with a thud, urgency in every step. He stood over the man that was sent to kill him and watched him fight for air, gurgling on his own blood.

"The fuck you thought, nigga," East boiled with rage. He leaned over snatching Flaco up slightly off the ground by his shirt. Enough to press the gun to his forehead then fired a single shot. The bullet lodged into Flaco's brain and his eyes suddenly became vacant. There was no more gurgling, no more gasping, only silence. East stared down at the body of a person he had called a friend. Shit was way out of hand and he no longer knew who to trust. Friend or foe, the lines didn't exist anymore. For him, they had become one in the same. It was time to put his own plan in motion.

CHAPTER TWENTY-FIVE

The next day, East pulled up to Ricardo's home. When Lauryn opened the door, her words got caught in her throat. She hadn't seen him since they had kissed at the cemetery weeks earlier. She had tried her best to put the kiss out of mind but seeing him brought it all back. Her hands became clammy as butterflies fluttered in her stomach. She normally was the one to have that effect on men, but the tables had been turned on her. She felt nervous in his presence and looked away from his gaze. She led him out to the back of the house where Ricardo sat at a table poolside.

Ricardo with the help of his cane, slowly rose to

his feet to shake East's hand and give him a hug then returned to his seat.

"How you feeling?" East asked.

"I've been better, but I've been worse too," Ricardo laughed.

"I got something that I think will make you feel a lot better," East said.

"What's that? I like surprises as long as they are the good kind," Ricardo's face brightened with anticipation.

"I can show you better than I can tell you," East explained then helped Ricardo to his feet.

He guided Ricardo out to the front of the house, where his car was parked. East went to the rear of the car and opened the trunk. Inside, there was a dark skin man in his late twenties. His wrists and ankles had been hogtied. His mouth duct taped. He was squirming around trying to free himself. When Blue saw Ricardo and East stalking over him, his face turned ashen white and his eyes grew as wide as an eight-lane highway.

"I think this is the man who shot you. And I think you'll want to hear what he has to say," East announced.

"It wasn't him. It was his brother," Ricardo said and up until then he hadn't revealed that he had actually seen who shot him. "But he will do for now," he had a devilish grin. He was going to enjoy killing Blue. Finally, he would have a taste of vengeance. His adrenaline seemed to give him the strength he needed to complete his mission. Three weeks ago, there had been an attempt made on his life. He had been shot five times outside the boxing gym he owned but luckily, he survived. Although, there were still two bullets lodged in his back, Ricardo was starting to get used to dealing with the constant pain that radiated through his body from the remaining slugs. He no longer could move with the same graceful fluidity he once had. That was still taking some time to get used to. Along with the fact that his body felt like it had aged a full decade overnight. Five bullets ripping through you would do that to anybody. He was still a little paranoid, wearing a bulletproof vest under his grey Nike tracksuit as he stood in his driveway. Ricardo's dark eyes were cold and filled with murderous intent. His mind playing over the savage physical violence he planned to inflict on the Blue. Twisted scenarios of torture slowly moved through his head, like hungry sharks around a bleeding man. Until he had revenge, Ricardo would not be healed physically or mentally, just a broken shell of the man he once was. His eyes widened with excitement and anticipation. He had to refrain from killing Blue right there.

"I got a place we can take him," he looked over at East and smirked. East nodded and slammed the truck closed.

Lauryn watched from the bedroom window in a panic as she listened to their conversation. When she saw them drive away in East car, she quickly dialed Dos' number. She paced back and forth in the middle of the bedroom. His phone seemed to ring forever before he picked up.

"What's good ma," he answered calmly.

"Nothing is good. Nothing at all,' she cried into the phone.

"Whoa, hold up. What's going on?" he asked.

"East just came here with somebody tied up in his truck. I think it was that guy, Blue," she whispered the last part like someone was listening in on their conversation.

"What!" Dos was now in a slight panic, but he tried masking it to keep her calm. "You sure?"

"Yes. They just left together. Oh shit, we're dead Dos," she wanted to throw up instead she began to cry harder.

"Calm down. I'm gonna figure this shit out."

"No," she screamed. 'It's nothing to figure out.

We have to leave."

"Leave?"

"Yes. We have to get out of town, or your father is going to kill us. Urrgh," she shouted in frustration. She should have never got in cahoots with Dos.

Although he hated to admit it, the safest place to be for the both of them was out of town. At least, until he could find a way to fix things. "Ok. Ok. Let me think," he said.

He was taking too long for her liking. She was the one in immediate danger. Ricardo could comeback at any moment and kill her. "I'm leaving Dos. With or without you," she said.

"You right ma. You should get the fuck out of there, right now," Dos admitted. Grab what you can and get in your car. I'll meet you somewhere."

Lauryn was already packing. Stuffing a few important things into her designer carry-on bag. "There is a motel by the airport. You know the one."

"Yeah," he said. "I'll meet you there in a half hour," he promised.

"Dos, if you don't show—" she started but he cut her off.

"I'll be there," he assured her.

"If you're not, I'm leaving without you," she said then hung up the phone. She raced frantically around the room grabbing things then headed for her car.

* * *

From the spot in the middle of the floor where he lay writhing in pain, Blue could hear shoes across the darkness. Suddenly Ricardo Wheeler emerged from the shadows of the warehouse carrying something in his hand that Blue couldn't quite make out. He walked with a heavy limp. His eyes were dark and cold when he reached Blue, he sat the bright red gas can down. He knelt down beside him and pulled the duck type from his mouth. Blue immediately spit in his face, hoping it would anger Ricardo enough to put him out of his misery. There was no such chance of that happening.

Ricardo took out a handkerchief from his pocket and wiped his face clean. He rose to his feet and swung his head side to side, cracking his neck. He pulled the gun from his waist. He looked at the black .45 in his hand but gripping a loaded pistol had long lost its excitement. He wasn't there for thrills. He was there for revenge. His blood warmed to the thought of that. Every muscle in his body began to tingle. He was a pro at the top of his game. Standing over Blue, he felt at the height of his power. How dare someone test his position, he thought to himself then he kicked

Blue in the stomach.

Ricardo looked at his victim's grimacing face. The smell of fear was in the air. "What made you niggas think you could come for my crown?" The high that came from having power was like a drug. It sent a euphoric feeling through his body numbing his own pain from head to toe. "Now look at you." He put the gun next to Blue's ear and pulled the trigger. The loud noise echoed through the warehouse.

"Ahhh," Blue screamed in excruciating pain. His ear drum had been busted and blood leaked from his ear. The loud ringing in his head went on for minutes. Blue began to struggle to free himself, to no avail. He looked like an animal trying to break its restraints. His constant moans and pleas fell on deaf ears. Ricardo planned to make an example out of him. The next person would think twice before making a move on him. He had to restore order in the streets. Reestablish the pecking order in Miami's underworld. He picked up the gas can that sat at his feet and began pouring gasoline over Blue's body and head. "Not like this, please!" Blue wailed in terror.

"No, I think this is perfect," Ricardo said. "What you think East?" he asked looking off to the side where he was standing. East nodded. "Tells everyone who's still in charge. I think my message will be very clear," Ricardo continued. He reached in his pocket and removed a cigar. He put it in his mouth and lit it.

Blue shouted, "No! Not like this!" as Ricardo began to puff on the cigar. "This wasn't me or my brother's idea. My brother was hired to kill you."

The statement intrigued Ricardo causing him to hesitate. He looked over at East.

"I think you might wanna hear this part," East informed him.

"Hired by who?" Ricardo commanded to know.

"Your son," Blue revealed.

"Dos? Nigga please," Ricardo's hearty laugh filled the spacious warehouse. "No way my son had anything to do with this."

"I have no reason to lie to you. I know I'm going to die. I have nothing to gain. Just thought you should know."

"Bullshit," Ricardo challenged.

"How'd you think my brother knew exactly where you'd be that early in the morning?" Blue asked. "Who were you supposed to be meeting with?"

The question was so heavy it felt as though Ricardo's chest would collapse from absorbing it into his heart. Because he knew the answer. It was one he didn't want to accept. The rage that burned in his eyes for Blue began to dim quickly before faded completely. Doused by the hurt and betrayal he suddenly felt. His soul was crushed into broken shards of glass. This was something he would have never expected. No man could fathom that his own seed, his flesh and blood, his one true heir, could be capable of such disloyalty. He had been betrayed in the most painful way. Ricardo always had his eye on everyone within his organization except the one person he should've been watching. The person he would've never thought to keep under close observation. The person closest to him, closest to his heart. Dos had done the unthinkable. In return, Ricardo was left with the hardest choice he would ever have to make in his life. He knew in his heart there really was no other choice but what hurt the most was knowing he didn't have the heart to do it himself. Ricardo let a single tear fall from his eye then he tossed the lit cigar on to Blue, instantly sending him up in flames. As he watched him burn, Ricardo felt East's comforting hand on his shoulder.

"You believe him?" East asked somberly.

Ricardo slowly nodded his head in confirmation. "I was supposed to meet Dos that morning, but he never showed," he admitted reluctantly, every word drenched in sadness.

"Where'd he say he was?" East inquired.

"He said, he had overslept. Something about fucking two bitches the night before," Ricardo said.

"C'mon, let's get out of here," East said, helping Ricardo to the car. His adrenaline had worn off and he was feeling the pain. Physically and emotionally.

* * *

Dos stepped out his car and walking over to the car that was waiting in front of the motel for him. Lauryn was inside. When she spotted him, she folded her arms over her chest. A look of fear and irritation spread across her face.

"It's about time. What took you so long?" she cried nervously. "Why weren't you answering my calls," Lauryn fumed as she stared at him from inside her car. She didn't like being in the dark on his plan.

"I'm here now. Don't nothing else matter. We got to figure this shit out," he declared.

Lauryn was tapping on the steering wheel and biting the inside of her cheek. "You think this is really gonna work?" she questioned nervously. The fear of the unknown had caused doubt to creep into her mind. She knew what was at stake, their life was on the line. She was willing to risk it all to escape Ricardo's authoritative manner.

"Relax ma," Dos told her. "Where's the money

and bricks?"

"In the trunk," she replied.

"Open the trunk," he stated calmly. Lauryn did as she was told. Dos walked to the back of the car and removed the duffel bag. He slammed it shut. He emerged from behind the car and motioned for her to get out as well. He rubbed his fingers through her hair. It was a soothing gesture, he tried to put her mind at ease. "I need you to relax."

"I'm just paranoid," she admitted as she nervously bit the skin off her bottom lip.

"I got it under control. You don't have to worry no more," Dos smiled, pulling her to him and kissing her lips. Lauryn's heart skipped a beat as she processed Dos' words, for many years that was all she wanted, she wanted the captivity to be gone. She wanted to know that Ricardo would be six feet under and no longer able to control her. Lauryn would finally get her life back. Strangely, she felt a hint of guilt in her heart, knowing that she would play a part in taking someone's life. She may not be the one to pull the trigger, but it would be like she had done it herself. The feeling surfaced and passed all in an instant. Lauryn would wear this as a badge of honor, fulfilling the promise she made to her late father every time she visited his grave. *He's gonna pay for it all daddy,* she thought as they reached to door of the motel room.

CHAPTER TWENTY-SIX

Ricardo sat alone at the desk in his home office, feeling sick to his stomach. He couldn't watch any longer. He pointed the remote at the TV and cut it off. He now knew the reason for his son's betrayal. The love and affection of a woman; his woman.

After returning home with East, he found Lauryn gone along with many of her things. He also found his safe wide open. She had cleaned him out. Taking all the money and bricks she could find. He was sure then that she was in on everything with Dos. He checked the tapes from the security cameras and there she was taking everything she could before vanishing.

Ricardo's thoughts were in shambles. He had been betrayed by two of the people he loved most. He wondered if they had been intimate, in his home. He checked the hidden camera no one knew about. What he saw broke him. Dos and Lauryn fucking in his bedroom while he lay in a coma in the hospital. Lauryn's ass propped up in the air, on their bed as his son pounded her relentlessly from behind. Ricardo tossed the half empty glass of Cognac across the room. The tiny hairs on his neck stood up. Fury took over his entire body. His breathing pattern quickened, and he became hot, beads of sweat forming on his forehead. "I'm going to enjoy killing that bitch. I should've fed her and her father to the sharks," he reminisced about that faithful day on the yacht, years ago.

He had other plans for his son. Ricardo knew he could never curl the trigger on his on seed, even after all the disloyalty. He got up from behind the desk and walked slowly in the living room, where East was on the phone pacing back and forth. He was trying to locate Dos and Lauryn's whereabouts.

"Ok, thanks. I owe you my nigga," East said as he ended a phone call. He looked at Ricardo and could see the pain in his face. He could only imagine what he must have been feeling inside. "I know where they are," East revealed. "My man said, he spotted their cars at some low budget, crackhead motel by the airport.

"They trying to lay low and get out of town." Ricardo said.

"Where would they go?" East asked.

"California, probably," Ricardo said. "Dos' mother lives out there," he revealed. "C'mon, let's go take care of this," Ricardo didn't sound excited at all by what he had to do. He turned to East as they made it to the door. "You know, you're my only son now," Ricardo said grabbing him by the shoulders with tears in his eyes.

Ricardo sat in silence as they drove. He couldn't help but to compare Dos and East and think about how they had turned out. He was truly amazed at what East had become. He was even sharper than he thought. Plus, he was honorable. At that moment, Ricardo wished that East was his own son. From the day he walked into the boxing gym, Ricardo knew he was destined for greatness. Ricardo had an eye for talent. He could spot a kid and know exactly how to use him within his organization for his own benefit. He truly couldn't bring himself to murder his own son, but East had proven, that he could do what most couldn't. He could kill despite emotion.

"Some things might need to be done tonight, that I might not necessarily be comfortable with having to do," Ricardo confessed as they drove.

"I understand," East replied. "Don't worry, I got you," he assured Ricardo. The look in his eyes matched his words.

Ricardo was relieved. His hands would remain clean although his heart would forever be stained. *Ungrateful bastard*, he thought to himself about Dos right as they turned into the motel parking lot.

It didn't take long to spot the cars. They were the most expensive ones in the parking lot and stuck out like an ink spot in milk.

"Look, there they go," East said, pointing to the two vehicles. "They gotta be in that room right there."

They parked and got out. They didn't say a word to each other as they walked towards the door. Each man was filled with so many thoughts and emotions. They were there to kill, they both knew it, but it didn't make it any easy. Both had performed the task of murder before but tonight there was an unfamiliar heaviness in their hearts. A weight on their shoulders that made the concrete seem to buckle underneath each step they took.

Ricardo removed the gun from his waist. East

already had his out. From outside the door they could hear the TV blaring. It sounded like SportsCenter. Ricardo took a deep breath as East knocked heavily on the door. After a few moments it opened, slowly but Ricardo didn't wait. He pushed himself into the room, gun raised, followed closely by East.

What Ricardo saw made him hesitate to shoot. Dos was tied to a chair, wearing only a bloodied wife beater and boxer briefs. His face was swollen and bruised from the tremendous beating he had suffered. He was bleeding from a gash in his head and his mouth was duct taped.

"What the fuck?' Ricardo said before he felt a thud to the back of his head and the world faded to black.

* * *

When Ricardo came to, he was still inside the motel room. It was still spinning as he tried to focus. His blurry vision slowly cleared and then his heart sunk. East stood with his gun at his side, next to a tied- up Dos. While Screw and Ques had their guns trained on Ricardo himself.

"You know before Tez died, he told me the whole story about what really happened to my father. He said when it was time to take care of him for snitching, you couldn't pull the trigger yourself and he had to do it for you. I respected him for telling me the truth," East recalled. "I barely knew my father, so it didn't really bother me, but I loved Tez," East said from his heart.

Ricardo was starting to get an idea of what this was about. Confidence could be a weakness if it exceeds its limit. Ricardo had first underestimated Dos and now he had done the same with East. This time it would prove to be a fatal mistake.

"You did the same thing to me with Tez. You couldn't kill him yourself, so you made me do it. Even tonight, with all the, "You my only real son now," shit. You were trying to get me to do your dirty work when it came to Dos." East shook his head, putting his hand on Dos shoulder. A sympathetic gesture, even if he truly had none for him.

"Eastwood, let me explain," Ricardo tried speaking but East was having none of it. He was in control.

"Ain't nothing to explain. You can't talk your way out of this one," East promised then he walked over to him. "Kill Dos," he instructed, the same way Ricardo had done to him, that night in the gym. He handed Ricardo his own gun back. "And before you even think about it, there's only one bullet in there,"

East stated.

Ricardo began to cry like a child at the choice he had been given. When he didn't move fast enough, East's looked at Screw, who walked over and put a gun to Ricardo's head.

"You remember how this goes, right? It's either him or you," East repeated the words Ricardo had once told him.

Ricardo had ordered him to kill so effortlessly that night but now he couldn't do the deed himself. He wept as he walked over to Dos. He lifted the gun. His hand was unsteady, trembling uncontrollably. Tears ran down his face, but his finger remained paralyzed, unable to curl on the trigger. "Please Eastwood. Don't make me do this," he pleaded.

Dos looked up into his father's eyes. The man he had tried to have killed only a few weeks prior. Now presented with the same opportunity his father couldn't kill him. He felt like the lowest of lows. Seeing the agony on his father's face, made Dos hurt more for him than he did himself. He began to sob equally as hard as Ricardo.

"Please East," Ricardo begged. "It has to be another way we can make this right."

"Ain't no other way." He was stone faced. Unwavering in his demand. He drew his gun as Que turned up the volume of the TV.

Ricardo head fell in defeat as his shoulders slumped. All his powerful aura and bossed up swag deflated. He lifted his head and raised the gun, gradually. The weapon seemed to weigh a thousand pounds in his hand. He pressed the gun to Dos' forehead.

"Dad no, please," Dos begged.

Ricardo looked away.

"Look a man in the eyes, when you send him to God," East taunted he jammed his gun into Ricardo's jaw and pushed his head straight ahead again.

Ricardo cried harder. "I love you son. I'm sorry," were his last words to Dos. Then he pulled the trigger, sending a single bullet through his brain. The force slumped Dos' whole body over in the chair.

Ricardo cried hysterically staring down at his son's dead body. East put his gun to the back of Ricardo's head. He closed his eyes and waited for the bullet that would end his life. Without hesitation, East curled his finger on the trigger. Ricardo's body collapsed to the floor with a heavy thud.

East looked around at the bodies of father and son. He had finally got his revenge, but he didn't feel the need to celebrate. Surprisingly, he felt nothing, no joy, no happiness or sadness. His face remained expressionless. He just nodded. The deed was done. He exited the motel room, leaving Screw and Que to take care of the bodies. Ricardo's run was over, and Dos' was too before it ever got started.

* * *

East entered his apartment and noticed a black duffel bag sitting on the coffee table in the middle of the living room. He pulled out his gun and scanned the room. He wasn't for any more surprises. He quickly searched the apartment making sure he didn't have any unwelcomed company. When he was satisfied that the apartment was empty. He walked over to the bag and unzipped it.

His eyes widened in surprise. There had to be at least a dozen sparkling, white bricks inside with a note resting on the top. He picked it up. It was from Lauryn. It read: Thank you for all your help. This should get you started. When you're done, call this number. He'll be expecting you. Then there was a lipstick kiss, followed by 7 digits scribbled at the bottom. Underneath the number was the name, Navarro.

LOVE SELDOM. TRUST NEVER.

THE END.

ABOUT THE AUTHOR

Hailing from Peekskill, NY, Ty Marshall is a refreshing voice in crime fiction. An undeniable talent with a highly skilled pen that speaks to the streets. He is widely considered one of the rising African American authors in the country and has enjoyed independent success with several releases through his own company, Marshall House Media. Please visit his website for news & updates:

www.tymarshallbooks.com

MORE

TY MARSHALL BOOKS

KEYS TO THE KINGDOM 1
KEYS TO THE KINGDOM 2
KINGDOM COME
80'S BABY: WHEN CRACK MADE KINGS
GOLD BLOODED
EAT, PREY & NO LOVE

CPSIA information can be obtained
at www.ICGtesting.com
Printed in the USA
FSHW010845120520
70131FS

9 780998 441979